A MOST CURIOUS CHRISTMAS

KATHERINE BLACK

BLOODHOUND
BOOKS

For JNB and NRB
My very first partners in crime

CHAPTER 1

HERE WE COME A-WASSAILING

May Morrigan stood at her library window, sipping her lapsang souchong while watching her sister doing yoga on the heath. In the corner of the room, beneath the spiral staircase to the gallery, the white lights of the Christmas tree twinkled. It was mid-December, with frost coating every surface, but Cass, out on the grass, was dressed in leggings and a light, zipped jacket. Cass Morrigan had spent most of her life in hot climes and dressed accordingly in bright, tropical colours that seemed to stick two fingers up at the grey English winter. She was like one of those vibrant feral parakeets often seen in Greenwich Park that had managed to escape captivity and miraculously thrive in the melancholy environment.

'She doesn't give a damn, does she?' Fletcher, May's housemate and oldest friend, joined her at the window with his mug of Earl Grey. They watched as a jogger swerved out of the way when Cass moved into downward dog. At almost seventy years old, her flexibility and balance were impressive. She looked younger than her age, though May was certain she'd had some assistance. Cass's breasts seemed unnaturally perky for a woman of her vintage. The years in America had left their mark.

May shook her head, watching as Cass stretched into a side plank. 'Here comes Geoffrey. This'll be good.'

They both leant closer to the window as May's neighbour, Geoffrey Crichton, a rising young MP, approached Cass on the grass.

'He thinks she's you.' Fletcher chuckled.

'She'll soon put him straight,' May said. They watched Geoffrey's face crease in confusion as he spoke with Cass. 'No, I was wrong,' May growled. 'She's pretending to be me. I can see it on her face. God knows what she's saying to him.' May slammed the mug down on her desk, sloshing tea across the surface.

Geoffrey scuttled off, leaving Cass with a smirk on her face. She tossed her short white hair and turned towards the house, a look of gratification visible even from that distance. May and Fletcher shrank back from the window.

'Why did Minty invite her to Greenway?' May said. 'I haven't seen Cass in decades, then she turns up out of the blue weeks before Christmas. She's only been here a few days and she's already irritating me. As if I don't have enough on my plate with the divorce. I don't need Minty's meddling.'

'You rang?' Minty said as she shuffled into the library. Araminta Morrigan, known as Minty, was a glorious ninety-six-year-old with a wonky blonde wig and a penchant for seventy-year-old toy boys. She was also May and Cass's mother. 'What have I done now?'

'Why on earth did you invite Cass?' May asked. 'And without asking me, I might add.'

'I don't need your permission to invite my own child here for Christmas. Greenway is still my home, Polly May Morrigan, at least until I die. Then, you may invite whomever you choose. Or not. Besides, this will probably be my last Christmas. I'd like to spend it with both of my daughters.' She shrugged, jingling the bracelets that lined her skinny arms.

'You've been saying it's your last Christmas for decades,' May replied. 'Yet, you're still here.'

'One could argue that the statement becomes increasingly accurate each year,' Minty said. 'So just shut your trap and make the best of it. Cass is here, and we're having a family Christmas *for once.*' She eased herself onto a chair in front of the fire.

May sighed. Greenway hadn't hosted a family Christmas since… May couldn't remember when. Her forty-year marriage to James hadn't produced any children, much to May's regret. Christmas had usually been a quiet, mournful time for May. She'd gone through the motions, organising a special lunch for the two of them and attending Midnight Mass, but it wasn't a particularly happy time. In the past, Cass had been in America, Minty had been in France, and Fletcher had had his life in Cambridge to keep him busy.

After James abruptly left May for another woman, Fletcher had come to live with her. He'd retired from teaching art history at the university, and they'd resumed a friendship forged in their youth. Then, Minty rocked up, saying she'd come home to die, causing May's life to take an unexpected detour. Surprisingly, it had all turned out to be a change for the better.

May's home, Greenway, a large Georgian house overlooking Blackheath in southeast London, felt full to bursting. It was a new, though not unpleasant, sensation. Maybe a Morrigan family Christmas wouldn't be the worst thing in the world.

'May Morrigan, you old floozy!' Cass bounded into the room laughing, pink-cheeked from cold and exertion. Fletcher jumped, almost spilling his tea as Minty giggled.

May's cautious bubble of optimism burst immediately.

May knew very well that she was far from being a floozy. The final decade of her marriage had been a cold, sexless charade, yet she'd remained faithful right up to the end. She'd recently started dating a charming local artist. Their time together was always reassuringly satisfying but could never be described as anything but monogamous. May Morrigan was in love. Perhaps.

'What have you done now?' May asked with a long sigh. Cass could irritate May just by breathing. When she actually made an effort at annoyance, it was intolerable.

Cass plopped down into the armchair across from Minty, throwing her legs over the armrest. 'That neighbour of yours couldn't get away fast enough when I suggested he join me in a half-moon asana. He thinks you're a cougar in heat.' She threw back her head and laughed. Fletcher cleared his throat and sipped his tea, eyes twitching back and forth between May and Cass.

May made a face. 'I see you haven't lost your sophomoric sense of humour.'

'Oh, unclench,' Cass said, rolling her eyes. 'He seems like a jackass anyway.' Cass's Americanisms grated on May's gentle ear.

Cass stretched extravagantly. 'Looks like there's some excitement on the heath this morning. Cops everywhere, men in CSI suits crawling all over the grass. I'm off for a shower.' She jumped up and left the room, creating an odd vacuum of silence and stillness with her exit. Cass had always had that effect. May sat down in the vacated armchair, suddenly exhausted.

May and Cass, christened Pollux May and Castor Kay Morrigan by a father fascinated with astrology, were identical twins. Though they shared the same DNA, Cass was like a technicolour version of May. She was like that scene in *The Wizard of Oz* when Dorothy opens the door to Oz, and the screen goes from black and white to full colour. Where May was elegant and outwardly restrained, Cass was relaxed and unfiltered. When they were both at Cambridge, Cass was the outspoken Katharine Hepburn to May's more feminine Audrey. She'd chain-smoked Rothmans, drank Double Diamond (none of that Babycham shite for Cass) and wasn't afraid to completely desecrate anyone who dared to challenge her on any topic. She was a free spirit who'd been married three or four times. May had stopped counting after the second one. Like May, Cass had never had children.

'I wonder what's happened on the heath,' Fletcher said. 'Shall we take a look?'

Minty wandered back towards her room as May and Fletcher grabbed their coats. May's two mini dachshunds, Bess and George, sensing an opportunity for a walk, scampered into the hall and started pulling at their leads on the hook by the door.

'Yes, yes,' May said to them. 'You're coming too.'

Fletcher opened the door to a brisk winter day. May's home overlooked the vast green of Blackheath.

In the summer, Blackheath Village morphed into a seaside town minus the sea. Sunbathers sprawled across the grass, picnics and parties dotted the expanse with blankets and kites. An ice-cream van was always parked outside the church and the local pubs served drinks in plastic cups so they could be taken out onto the green to be enjoyed in the sunshine. Sex on the Heath was a favourite summertime tipple created by an enter-prising local bar.

In the winter, the heath became a passing-through sort of place, full of dog walkers, joggers, and families trying to exhaust their children before bedtime. The vibrant green of the summer faded into a muted greige. Photographs of the heath in winter were always black and white, even when they weren't.

Every window and doorway at the front of May's home presented postcard-perfect views of the 211-acre park with the village perched off to the right and the church, St Julian's, taking centre stage. The church, surrounded by green on all sides, looked as if it had been dropped down onto the grass from a great height.

Once May and Fletcher had bundled up and made it out onto the heath, they spotted a crowd gathering around the Millen-nium Circle just north of Duke Humphrey Road. The Circle was a large, paved area at the intersection of two paths, laid to commemorate the 2012 London Olympics and the Queen's Diamond Jubilee. Why it was called The *Millennium* Circle was a mystery. A police tent had been erected in the centre of the paving stones, crime-scene officers coming and going in their white coveralls.

'Looks serious,' Fletcher said. He squinted at the scene. 'They always remind me of Oompa-Loompas in those get-ups. Ah, now this must be their Wonka.' An older man stalked into the crowd and began gesturing for the groups of residents milling around on the grass to move along, there was nothing to see.

'He certainly knows the script,' May replied.

The detective was about May's height and stocky, wearing a dark suit and a surprisingly bright striped scarf under his black wool coat. His ruddy face, with its shock of silver hair, turned towards May and Fletcher. The man looked weary, as if he'd been in the job far too long.

As people began to disperse, he made his way over. May and Fletcher were still watching events as the dogs sniffed the ground around them in search of fox trails.

'Move along, please,' he said. His tone was gruff, immediately putting May's back up.

'I live just around the corner,' May replied. 'I'd like to know what's happened. Are we in any danger?'

He shook his head. 'No more danger than anyone else in this godforsaken city. Please, move along. Now.'

Fletcher humphed.

'But what's happened?' May persisted. 'Tents like that are used for bodies, and you've got SOCO all over the place. Was someone killed?'

The detective sighed. 'SOCO, is it? This isn't *Midsomer Murders*, madam.'

'No, it's Blackheath,' May said. Had the man gone mad?

A trace of a smile changed his whole face. He was actually rather handsome. He looked at May, making some kind of inner calculation, then sighed. 'It seems to be a mugging gone wrong. A runner, early this morning, stabbed. No phone or wallet. We're working on identifying the victim now.'

'I've lived here my whole life and know most people,' May replied. 'Perhaps I can help with that.'

The detective looked around the heath as he thought it over. The common was busy with dog walkers and families walking their children to school at St Julian's Primary. May spotted a small child proudly toting a papier-mâché donkey's head across the grass, preparing for the school's nativity play.

'Okay,' the detective decided suddenly. 'One quick look. If you don't recognise him, just say. No nosing around the site.'

May and Fletcher moved forwards, but the detective stopped them.

'Just the lady,' he said. He pointed at Fletcher. 'You stay here with the mutts.'

Fletcher huffed but did as he was told. May trotted off after the detective, turning to stick her tongue out at Fletcher, left behind pouting on the grass.

The centre of the Millennium Circle felt like a portentous place to die. As they approached, the busy bees working the crime scene stilled and parted, allowing May and the detective through. A minion handed May a pair of plastic shoe covers. She paused to slip them on. The detective leant forwards and spoke to her in a low voice. 'Are you sure about this? You can back out. That's fine. I'm only allowing you to look because I'd like to be able to notify the next of kin as soon as possible. It's a young man, in his forties, I'd guess. He probably has a family who are worried sick this morning.'

May nodded. 'I'm sure,' she said. 'It's not my first rodeo.' She took a deep breath and stepped inside.

CHAPTER 2

IT'S BEGINNING TO LOOK A LOT LIKE
CHRISTMAS

Fletcher checked his watch again. That detective had been rather rude. What did it matter if Fletcher stood outside the tent while May had a look at the body? It was just plain old bloody-mindedness on the part of the police. Fletcher took a step closer to the crime scene. The heath was a public space after all. He took another step. Who was this detective to tell Fletcher he couldn't walk in a public park? The nerve of some people. Fletcher took another step forwards.

A young police constable caught Fletcher's eye and made a shooing motion. Fletcher raised a foot to step forwards in defiance. He'd broken through the police lines in Grosvenor Square in '68, for God's sake. He wouldn't be told what to do on his own bloody doorstep.

The PC stepped forwards. Fletcher quickly retreated, but he gave the constable a look he wouldn't soon forget.

Fletcher wasn't due at the theatre until ten, but he'd hoped to go over his notes from the previous day and take some time to prepare before entering the lion's den. May needed to hurry up. How long did it take to identify a corpse?

Fletcher had been flattered when he was first asked to write a

Christmas panto for the Blackheath Players. Margaret Stout, head of the Players, had approached him one summer day while he was languid and laughing in the beer garden at the Princess of Wales pub. He'd agreed at once and started brainstorming ideas with his partner, Sparks.

Sparks. Fletcher missed him desperately. Sparks, AKA Gerald Chanda, was a semi-retired computer science teacher and boyfriend *extraordinaire*. Sparks was handsome and hairy. He gardened. He cooked. He kept bees and produced the most delicious honey. He was a part-time inventor and full-time sweetheart, but Sparks was spending the Christmas break in Chennai, visiting his extended family. He'd asked Fletcher to accompany him ('You'll collect some great material for your next book.'), but Fletcher knew that May would need him over the holidays with both her mother *and* sister in the house.

Besides, by the time Sparks had made his travel arrangements, Fletcher was already knee-deep in panto. It would be his glorious return to the theatre, this time as playwright rather than performer. A triumphant moment to commemorate his memorable performance as Widow Twankey when he and May had been part of the Cambridge Footlights during their uni days.

Margaret Stout knew when she was onto a good thing. Not only had she persuaded Fletcher to write the play, she'd also talked him into directing it *and* convinced him that getting the one and only Clark Wolfe to play the Dame would be an absolute coup. A coup that only Fletcher, with his charm and connections, could possibly accomplish. Fletcher, utterly defenceless when it came to flattery, had agreed to do his best.

Clark Wolfe had performed with Fletcher in the Footlights when they were all at Cambridge in the sixties. Of course, he'd been plain old Milton Smellie back then. For May and Fletcher, the Footlights had been a bit of fun before they set off on their career paths as a librarian and a professor of art history. Milton, on the other hand, had abandoned his economics course in the middle of the year, dropped out of Cambridge, and changed his name to the more beguiling Clark Wolfe in order to pursue acting full time. He'd wormed his way into the hearts of most Brits playing the awkward, charming bungler in every role he took on. But he never quite managed to crack the all-important American market, even after spending a fortune having his teeth fixed.

To Fletcher's surprise and delight, Clark had agreed, for a nominal fee, to come and star in Blackheath's Christmas pantomime staged in the small theatre tucked behind the Age Exchange. His delight soon turned to remorse once Clark arrived, vividly reminding Fletcher why he'd never bothered to keep in touch. On top of being an irredeemable lech, he had an annoying habit of quoting *Monty Python* at any opportunity. Fletcher, May and Clark had briefly crossed paths with John, Eric and Graham at Cambridge, but Clark acted as if he'd been one of the founding members of the comedy troupe.

Thankfully, the show would run for one night only, just after the traditional village procession on Christmas Eve. Then Fletcher could return to his pleasant, theatre-free life.

He checked his watch and looked over his shoulder. Fletcher couldn't shake the feeling that someone was watching him. May was taking her time with that detective. Calling the dogs, he clipped on their leads, then stood dithering on the grass. They were less than a hundred metres from Greenway. He turned to admire the imposing house overlooking the heath, spotting Minty at the library window, staring into the distance like a ghostly apparition. She looked like the White Lady, foretelling death, or the Bell Witch, knocking on walls and hissing scripture. As if reading his thoughts, Minty's head slowly turned to look directly at Fletcher. He shivered under her gaze.

'All done,' May said, causing him to jump.

'Jesus,' Fletcher said. 'You scared the life out of me.' He put his hand to his chest, looking back towards the house. Minty had disappeared. May looked pale and slightly shaken. 'Was it very awful?' he asked.

'Come on,' she said. 'I need a drink.'

In the warmth of May's bright kitchen, Fletcher poured them each a mug of hot chocolate, adding a splash of whisky. He cut generous wedges of the good panettone from the Italian deli in Lewisham and slathered them with butter. Then they took their usual seats across from each other at the scrubbed pine table. Fletcher nibbled panettone, giving May time to gather herself before asking, 'Did you know him?'

She nodded, then took another sip of hot chocolate. 'It's Caspar Campbell, Harold Lambert's son-in-law.'

Fletcher's chest ached on hearing the news. Caspar and his wife, Jocasta, were a sweet couple who'd met later in life and started a family almost immediately. Their little daughter was an absolute delight. 'Poor Tansy,' Fletcher said. 'And Jo and Harold. The whole family will be devastated. He was a lovely man.' Fletcher could picture Caspar on the heath the previous summer with Tansy strapped to him in a baby carrier, her little strawberry-blonde head resting against his chest. 'What happened?'

May shrugged. 'They think it was a mugging. No watch, phone or any identification on him.' She shook her head. 'It's a very public place for an attack like that, right in the middle of the heath.'

Fletcher could almost see the gears turning in May's brain. 'You think it wasn't a mugging?'

May shook herself. 'I don't know. It just seems odd. And the wound… he was stabbed in the stomach. Just once, as far as I could tell. If it was a mugging, wouldn't they just threaten him, take anything valuable and run? Why stab him?'

'Maybe he fought back,' Fletcher said.

She shook her head. 'No defensive wounds that I could see.'

Fletcher scratched his head. 'Was there a note left behind? Perhaps with a riddle? An obscure reference to music or literature?'

May shook her head.

'An initial written in blood on the pavement?' Fletcher asked. 'Or maybe a scrap of paper with writing on it, concealed in the palm of the dead man's hand?'

'No,' May said. 'Nothing like that.'

'Now, that is peculiar.' He took a bite of panettone.

Cass banged into the kitchen, hair wet from the shower, and started assembling fruits and vegetables for a morning green juice. 'Did you get to the bottom of it?' she asked from deep in the fridge.

'The bottom of what?' May said, scowling at Cass's back.

Cass had made herself right at home in Greenway, as if she'd never left, filling May's fridge with "superfoods" and monopolising the washing machine with her workout clothes on a daily basis. Fletcher almost missed the hard-drinking, chain-smoker Cass used to be.

'The excitement on the heath,' Cass replied, spooning mysterious powders into the blender. 'As if you weren't nosing around out there the second I left the room. We're twins, remember? I know you better than you know yourself and I bet you were out there like a shot, annoying the police, meddling where you don't belong.' She started chopping apples and mint. 'You've probably got your own ideas about what happened, and I would bet a million dollars that you're making plans to get involved and puzzle it out all by yourself.' She turned and pointed the knife at May. 'Tell me I'm wrong.'

Fletcher hid his smile behind the mug of hot chocolate.

CHAPTER 3

HOLLY JOLLY CHRISTMAS

'*D*on't point that thing at me,' May said.

Cass turned back to the chopping board as May held two fingers up to her smug back.

'I saw that,' Cass said, shoving spinach, fruit and ice into the blender, then whizzing it up for what seemed an excessively long time.

'I don't know how you drink that stuff,' Fletcher said, watching Cass pour the khaki-coloured mixture into a tall glass.

She glugged it down in one, then wiped her mouth with the back of a hand. 'Best thing for you. Keeps you young. And regular.'

May rolled her eyes. She'd heard far too much about Cass's diet and exercise regime over the last few days. What would Cass expect for Christmas lunch? Kale and beans? They certainly had enough kale in the refrigerator. May absolutely drew the line at tofurkey. Not at her Christmas table.

The more Cass talked about whole grains and lean proteins, the more May found herself pulling the tin of Cadbury Roses chocolates out from under the sofa for some secret scarfing. She was certain that Fletcher had found her stash. The last time she'd looked, all of the hazelnuts in caramel were gone. They were his favourite.

Cass rinsed her glass and popped it in the dishwasher. 'I'm going into the village to do some shopping. Got a spare magnifying glass? I can look for clues. Maybe interview a few suspects.'

'I'll tell you what you can do...' May started.

Fletcher looked up, knowing very well what was coming.

Cass knew it too. She rushed out of the kitchen, smiling, before May could finish her sentence.

It was frustrating to be left hanging like that. May closed her eyes. 'I swear to God, Fletch. I cannot be held accountable for my actions when it comes to Cass.'

'You and Minty were much the same when she first arrived,' he said. 'And now look, she's good as gold.' He paused. 'Well, she's better than she was.'

'Are you saying that *I'm* the common denominator?' May gave Fletcher a look that made him sit further back in his seat.

'No, not at all,' he soothed. 'I'm saying the Morrigan genes are the common denominator. Three Morrigan women under one roof, it's a wonder the village hasn't been besieged by plagues or showered with frogs. It's like living with a bloody coven.'

May smiled. 'You do talk nonsense,' she said. 'But I take your point. I think Minty, Cass, and I are at our best in solitude.' She looked at Fletcher. 'If I'm a witch, what does that make you? My familiar?'

Fletcher peered at the dachshunds lolling on their bed beside the warm Aga. 'I think that role has already been sufficiently fulfilled.' He turned back to May. 'Has James come to his senses yet and dropped the court proceedings?'

She shrugged and flopped her arms at her sides. 'I haven't heard a peep, but then I did stop reading the emails. It's all such nonsense. There's no way he can claim any part of Greenway. The trust is watertight. He's not a Morrigan. He refused to take my name. I really don't understand why he's even trying. It's a complete waste of time and money.'

Fletcher nodded. 'I think he's just taking pleasure in forcing you to do something you don't want to do. He has no power over you now, except by making you face him in court. He's a small, petty man.' He sipped his hot chocolate before continuing. 'It's been a long time since you saw each other. Not since the day he left, and that was almost two years ago.'

'Yes,' May nodded, 'it's been a pleasant reprieve, but I guess all things must come to an end.' She banged the table. 'God, I resent the fact that he still has the power to upset me. All those years of training me to dance to his tune didn't go to waste. One shitty message from his solicitor and I'm right back in the black abyss of the marriage.' She closed her eyes as she continued. 'Minty has insisted on coming with me if we go to court. She's decided to suddenly act like a mother for once.' May sighed. 'Though I suppose there's some justification for her being there as the legal owner of Greenway. If nothing else, she'll be a distraction.'

Fletcher reached across the table and placed his hand over May's. 'I'm sorry I haven't been around lately. This panto has taken over my life. Oh, bugger! I'm late.' He jumped up from the table and started to leave the room, then hurried back to place his mug in the dishwasher before dashing out the door. 'We'll talk about this more later.' He popped back in, kissed the top of May's head, then was gone.

May remained in her chair, staring at the warped grain of the tabletop. She would go and see Harold Lambert, see if there was anything she could do for him or the family. She ran a hand across the uneven surface, thinking for the thousandth time in fifty years that it really needed to be re-sanded.

How *did* she feel about possibly seeing James again?

Sad? No, that wasn't it.

Nervous? No, not nervous. Or… maybe a little.

Irritated? Yes, she definitely felt irritated. He'd left her for another woman. May had been devastated, but with Fletcher's help, she'd healed. She was happier than she'd been in years. She'd even started dating, then James began all the nonsense about taking his share of Greenway and barged back into her life as if he was still entitled to it. It was so unnecessary. The divorce could've been simple, if not completely amicable. But no, James had to cause as much fuss as possible.

Furious? Yes, she was bloody furious. The nerve of the man. He'd been a complacent husband, at best. May realised she'd be quite happy to never lay eyes on him again. Yet here he was, trying to force her to appear in court, pressuring her to face him. How had she spent the bulk of her life with such a complete arse?

'What's got you all hot and bothered?' Minty asked as she bustled into the kitchen. 'Been watching *Peaky Blinders* again?' Minty leant against the kitchen sink. 'I dated a Brummie once. Absolute heaven. The things that man could do with his–'

'Yes, all right,' May interrupted. 'Thank you very much, Anaïs Nin. I'm not in the mood for your erotic reminiscences just now.'

Minty tutted and moved to refill the kettle. 'What's put the bee in your bonnet? You're worked up about something.'

May rubbed her face. 'Can you not figure it out? It looks like I'm about to be dragged into court by the entitled twat I married to finalise the last bit of this bloody divorce.'

Minty stopped what she was doing and turned to look at May. 'You've got nothing to worry about. There's no way James will get any kind of settlement regarding Greenway. You've gone through all the other financial nonsense. You're almost done with him. The priggish bastard is just wasting everyone's time.'

May smiled. Minty had said "bastard" with a strong Birmingham accent, and "priggish" was the perfect word to describe James. He had a habit of pursing his lips together when he disapproved of anything May said or did, which meant that he very frequently had a face like a cat's arsehole.

Even as she nursed him through his battle with colon cancer, he would press his lips together and look down at her in disgust. She could be holding sheets covered in his excrement after changing the bed linen and helping him wash, but if she tried to make a joke or lighten the mood, he would say she was being vulgar and shoo her from the room.

She blamed the behaviour on his sense of shame, but looking back she'd realised that it predated the cancer by many, *many* years. May had taught herself to tiptoe around James. She'd made herself smaller and smaller. It was only in the exhaustion of caring for him, when her internal guard was down, that she realised what an absolute pig's arse the man was. Still, she was willing to stick it out and make the best of things after so many years together. It was James who'd left her in the end.

'The divorce isn't what's bothering me…' May hesitated. 'Oh, it's stupid.'

'Go on.' Minty sat in Fletcher's chair across from May. 'Spit it out.' She had a concerned look on her face.

May could feel herself blushing, actually blushing! In a rush, she said, 'I don't know what to wear,' then sat back and folded her arms across her chest. 'There. I've said it. It's the end of my marriage, and I'm worrying about how I look for the priggish bastard who's divorcing me. What is wrong with me?'

Minty relaxed in the chair. 'Nothing's wrong with you, silly girl. You're human. Don't think for one minute that James Faraday won't be carefully choosing his outfit with you in mind. He's a vain old bastard. You just wear something you feel comfortable in. Get Fletch to help. He's good at that sort of thing.' She stood up and returned to her tea-making. 'And don't forget, I'll be right there beside you the whole time.'

Yes, May thought, *that's another thing that worries me.*

CHAPTER 4

HOME FOR THE HOLIDAYS

Cass burped. Christ, the smoothies were disgusting. Still, needs must. Drinking that shit was better than the alternative. The bloody yoga, the boring meditation. It all served a purpose, but what a fucking drag.

She lay down on the small double bed in her room, feeling exhausted. May had knocked upwards into their parents' bedroom to extend her library, then given two rooms to Fletcher to use as his bedroom and a small study. May had taken the biggest bedroom for herself while Minty had converted the front sitting room on the ground floor into a bedroom to avoid using the stairs. This left only the smallest room for guests. The space could barely fit the bed, a petite wardrobe and a bedside table. Everything in it was slightly shabby, the furniture bumped and worn at the edges, the quilts and sheets softened from hundreds of washes.

Cass turned her face into the pillow and inhaled deeply. It smelt of home. The pillows were probably the same ones she'd slept on as a teen. If she looked very carefully, would she find a 1960s peroxide-blonde hair trapped amongst the goose down?

Greenway was like a time capsule, housing old ghosts as well as the familiar fixtures and fittings. The bedside clock ticked off the seconds in soft clicks. It had once sat on her father's desk. Someone walked across the landing, causing the loose board to creak. The familiar sound made Cass painfully aware of the long passage of time since she'd last heard it. Was it better if *everything* changed or if it all remained the same?

She saw herself, a teenager, sneaking home in the middle of the night, carrying her shoes up the stairs, carefully avoiding the noisy floorboard so as not to wake Bertie and Minty. What would that young girl make of the woman Cass had become? Would she be proud? Horrified? Indifferent?

She closed her eyes, placed one hand across her chest and sighed.

Home. This was the place where Cass could soften, where she could stand down from life's battles and just *be*. If she could remember how to do those things.

May was the only person standing in her way, or rather there were things Cass needed to tell May before she could really let go of them. And she *would* tell May. Soon.

As she drifted off to sleep, something deep inside Cass Morrigan settled for the first time in decades.

CHAPTER 5

GOD REST YE MERRY GENTLEMEN

Fletcher entered the vestibule of the little Blackheath theatre in a rush. Voices could be heard inside the hall, the actors and dancers waiting for him impatiently, but he paused to take a moment to gather himself. Directing the panto had begun as an impulsive act of optimism, which quickly descended into a heavy daily burden. Managing Clark Wolfe topped the list of Fletcher's challenges, but there was more than one big personality in the company. Fragile egos came with the territory.

Most actors in a small theatre group felt it was just a matter of time before they were discovered and became stars. Without a doubt, the local production of *Peter Pan* would attract the likes of the next Kubrick or Scorsese, who would be spellbound by their performance. They all practised their Oscar and BAFTA speeches in the bathroom mirror. The really good ones fought back tears as they held the shampoo bottle aloft, thanking everyone, from that special teacher who made such a difference to dear Meryl for her generosity as an artist.

The truth was that only one out of thousands would ever be walking those red carpets. The rest would end up in repertory theatre, barely scraping by, if they were lucky. Most would end up languishing in boring office jobs that never came close to the thrill of the spotlight. Deep down, the performers knew this to be true. Their very justified fears created those enormous but fragile egos.

Fletcher took one last deep breath before pushing open the doors and entering the theatre proper. He was met by the congenial scents of wood, paint, dust and whispers of sweat that haunted the space from audiences and performers past. He strode down the aisle between the metal folding chairs set up for the children's performance of *The Nutcracker* later in the evening. The Players needed to leave the theatre by four that afternoon to make way for the toddlers in tutus.

The Blackheath Players were a small amateur company made up of an eclectic mix of young theatre students, local parents looking for an excuse to get out of the house, and OAPs who had a lot of time on their hands. A group of Players, dressed in spattered clothing, were painting trees onto soft flats for the Neverland scenes. Two dancers hopped about on stage, revelling in their youthful bodies and bountiful energy. Desi Meade was fitting a dress on Fletcher's Wendy, Malin Tanzer, while Clark Wolfe was seated on the front row, surrounded by a group of fellow actors, his eyes returning again and again to the young dancer playing Tinkerbell.

'Hugh is an absolute sweetheart,' he was saying. 'I did a few days on *Four Weddings*, and this whole idea that he's some kind of grump is just ludicrous.'

Fletcher remembered Clark's appearance in *Four Weddings and a Funeral*. He'd played a member of the congregation at one of the weddings. Fletcher suspected that "a few days" translated to something closer to "a few hours" and that his interactions with Hugh Grant were non-existent.

'Hugh is such a riot,' Clark continued. 'We've remained close, dear chap. He said the funniest thing at Annabel's nightclub the other night.'

'I thought he was making that new film in the States,' one of the older members piped up. 'The *Mail* had a photo of him this morning having a set-to with a paparazzo outside some ritzy restaurant.'

'I think Mr Wolfe would know better than you, Bob.' Louella Alard, the youngest dancer and Fletcher's Tinkerbell, was hanging on Clark's every word. 'Go on, Mr Wolfe,' she continued. 'Tell us what he said.'

Clark Wolfe's gaze lingered on Louella a beat too long before he opened his mouth to reply.

'All right, children.' Fletcher clapped his hands to get every-one's attention. 'Shall we begin?'

Clark scowled in Fletcher's direction, clamping his lips together, as the actors around him snapped to attention. '"You don't frighten us, English pig-dogs!"', he shouted.

It took Fletcher a moment to realise that he was quoting from Monty Python again. *God help us all.*

'"Go and boil your bottoms"', Clark continued. Then his eyes looked over Fletcher's shoulder and he pointed. 'No! You know the rules. Out!'

Fletcher turned just as the theatre doors shut. 'What was that all about?' he asked.

'Just my stalker,' Clark replied, loud enough so everyone could hear. 'Comes with stardom, unfortunately.'

Stalker, my arse. Clark was full of it.

'Fletcher,' Louella said, 'did you hear about the body on the heath? It must've happened this morning.' She shivered. 'So awful.'

Clark put his arm around her shoulders. 'Don't you worry, my dear. Stay close to me. Uncle Clark will keep you safe from harm.'

'Shall we start with the second act today?' Fletcher continued, ignoring Clark. 'That dance routine needs a bit of polish.'

Louella jumped up to join the other dancers. Clark Wolfe's unblinking gaze followed her across the room. Fletcher would need to keep an eye on that situation.

The dancers got into formation on the small stage, Louella at the front. Her tiny frame and pixie haircut were perfect for the role of the little fairy.

Fletcher took a seat next to Desi, who was sewing something sparkly in her lap. 'What do you think?' She held up the small, green, sequinned garment. It was Tinkerbell's outfit for most of the play.

'Desi, you're a wizard,' Fletcher replied. Desdemona Meade had been Costume Supervisor at the National Theatre for many years. She'd started her career as a dresser for the likes of Olivier, Mirren and Dench when they were all bright young things, working her way up to supervisor over the decades. Desi had retired many years previously but still volunteered her time to the Players. Fletcher was fascinated by her fine needlework. Desi wore enormous magnifying glasses when she was sewing but most often worked by touch, watching the rehearsals intently as her hands flitted about in her lap, forming stitches as accurately as any machine.

Like many costumiers, Desi herself was a work of art. Her once-red hair was dyed a vibrant pink and cut into a severe bob and fringe. The wisps floated around her head like a cap of flamingo feathers. She circled her eyes with kohl, adding turquoise shadow to the lids and a pink lipstick that matched her hair. Desi dressed in sumptuous and brightly coloured layers of fabric. Fletcher had never been able to identify an actual garment. She seemed to wrap herself in silks and velvets, ignoring any rules about mixing patterns or colours. Sometimes there would seem to be a theme, shades of lavender or all florals. More often than not, she dressed in a mishmash of whatever seemed to catch her eye that morning. Fletcher was reminded of Klimt's portraits of Adele Bloch-Bauer.

All these textiles were anchored in place with heavy necklaces, belts and bracelets made of metal, wood and plastic, with rings stacked on every finger. He couldn't imagine how she managed to sew with her hands so laden in jewellery. Fletcher thought that undressing for Desi must be like an archaeological dig, revealing herself layer by layer. The possibility of the bony, birdlike form encased within the layers flashed across Fletcher's mind, then he quickly focused his attention back onto the stage, thinking of Sparks's beefy, masculine body in comparison. He knew very well which one he would prefer to gaze upon.

'Well done, Louella,' Fletcher said. She'd stumbled a few times, but he could see that she was working hard to get it right. Louella had been a last-minute addition to the cast, recommended to the company by a friend when they found themselves without a suitable Tinkerbell. Fletcher had seen her carefully and consciously eating her sandwich at break, causing him to wonder if her small frame might be attributed to something besides genetics. She was a dear girl, and she was doing her best. At that level of theatre, Fletcher couldn't ask for more.

Clark pranced around the stage in his role as Widow Twankey. His exaggeratedly mincing movements and gestures put Fletcher's teeth on edge. But it *was* a panto, he reminded himself; hammy acting was the nature of the beast.

'Do I call you Tyrone Guthrie or Orson Welles?' May asked as she plopped herself down on the hard seat beside Fletcher.

'May! To what do I owe the honour?' It was the first time she'd attended one of the rehearsals. Fletcher wasn't sure if he was more delighted or embarrassed. It wasn't exactly a West End performance.

'Now that I'm seeing it, I think Peter Rogers might be more accurate,' she said, eyes following Clark onstage. 'What on earth does he think he's doing?'

Fletcher looked at Clark, who was doing something suggestive with a prop dagger. 'I'm beyond caring at this point. I just want to get the bloody thing over with.'

May greeted Desi, whom she'd known since childhood. Desi Meade and her husband, Hugo, were part of the scenery of Blackheath Village. They'd been a creative, slightly eccentric couple, adding a touch of vibrancy to the more traditional village charms. Hugo had been an artist, painting colourful abstract canvases or performing mind-boggling physical feats on camera for his more conceptual works. Sadly, Hugo had died decades before when a performance involving a tightrope and a series of chainsaws had gone horribly wrong.

'He died doing what he loved,' Desi would say with a lump in her throat. She'd never remarried.

Though years older, May had attended the same school as Desi's daughter, Dido, who'd been a late, though much-loved blessing to the quirky couple.

Fletcher, May and Desi sat in companionable silence as the rehearsal progressed. Fletcher would pause the action occasionally to make a suggestion, but the performers were mostly left to lurch through the dance routines and overact their way through the script. At last, he declared that everyone should take a break.

'That little dancer playing Tinkerbell is rather good,' May said. 'I'll maintain a courteous silence about the rest.'

Desi chuckled. 'You're a better woman than I,' she said. 'Fletcher's writing is clever, but it would take a better company than this to do it justice.' Her hands continued to twitch amongst the fabric in her lap.

Clark Wolf slid over to where they were sitting. Desi gathered herself and her tools and moved to speak to Louella.

'May Morrigan, as I live and breathe,' Clark said. He performed a dramatic bow, sprinkling May with sweat in the process.

May looked up at the man standing in front of her. 'Hello,

Milton,' she said. 'It's been a long time.' Fletcher tried not to smile at her cattiness.

Clark gave her a pitying look. 'It's Clark these days. Has been for some time, as you well know. Is the dementia setting in early, dear?' He leant down to pat May's arm, leaving a visibly damp mark, laughing as if he'd said something especially witty.

May curled her lip in distaste, cringing from him, then tried to turn the grimace into a polite smile. The attempt at diplomacy was less than successful.

'What's this I hear about a murder in charming Blackheath Village? Surely not.' Clark leered as if it was the punchline to a particularly dirty joke.

'There was a stabbing on the heath,' May replied in a monotone. 'It was a dear friend.'

Clark's face immediately switched to dramatic sadness and concern. 'May, I'm so sorry.' He reached out to pat her arm again, but May moved away just in time, scrubbing at the spot where he'd touched her before. Fletcher felt sick at Clark's display of false concern. Never trust an actor, especially a good one. Though admittedly, Clark was not a good actor.

'I think I'll go see Desi,' May said, standing and edging carefully out of Clark Wolf's reach, leaving Fletcher alone with him.

'Clark,' Fletcher said. 'I wonder if I could have a quick word with you.'

CHAPTER 6

IN THE BLEAK MIDWINTER

May shuddered beside Desi. 'That man is vile.' She shook herself again. 'Positively reptilian.'

'Hmph,' Desi agreed around the pins clamped between her teeth. She was kneeling down, carefully folding the edges of Louella's skirt, quickly pinning it in place for later hemming. May watched, mesmerised by Desi's hands, their speed and accuracy. Once the final pin was in place, Desi patted Louella on the bum saying, 'There you go, my dear. Just be careful of the pricklies.'

Louella twirled away to join the rest of the cast around the kettle as Desi turned to May, raising one arm. 'Give us a hand, love.'

May pulled Desi to her feet. Apart from the weight of fabric and accessories, there was nothing to her. The two women sat on chairs at the side of the stage. May watched Fletcher speaking to Clark. They seemed to be disagreeing about something, but the chatter and banging of the cast and stage crew drowned out their voices on the other side of the hall.

'How are you, Desi?' May asked. 'I hear you've moved into Demeter Gardens. They must be missing you on Chalcroft Road.'

Desi had lived in a little terraced house with a bright-yellow door for as long as May could remember. She'd organised the annual street party, roping in friends from the theatre to provide entertainment. The neighbours looked forward to it every June.

Desi nodded. 'Good old Dementia Gardens.' She sighed. 'It's fine. My rooms are comfortable. The staff are kind, and the food is edible. When one reaches my age, one loses so much of one's autonomy.' Desi looked at May. 'How is Minty doing? I understand she's back in Blackheath?'

May pursed her lips. 'Yes, Minty's back and driving me mad as ever. It's like having a teenager in the house.'

Desi chuckled. 'Sounds like the same old Minty.'

'You should come see her. You're just across the heath from us now.'

Desi had moved into the care home overlooking the heath. Demeter Gardens had once been a grand hotel, now redeveloped into a high-end home for the elderly. A portion of the building remained as a small boutique hotel where families could stay on their annual visit to granny and grandad to make sure they were still included in the will.

'I'd like that,' Desi said, as Fletcher clapped his hands and called everyone back to the stage.

'All right!' he said. 'Let's go again from the top of Act Two. Where's my crocodile?'

May strolled home across the heath. The December day was grey and overcast, much like her mood. She had a lot on her mind. There was the divorce. Her sister, Cass, in the house for the first time in years. Her mother, Minty, to contend with. And then there was Asa.

May had been dating Asa Oluso for almost six months. She supposed that what they were doing was dating, though it didn't always feel that straightforward.

Asa was a local artist. He painted abstract paintings that, at first glance, appeared to be blank canvases. On closer inspection, through cuts in the surface, the hidden layers underneath the white paint became visible. He'd first come to England as a young art student. When his paintings didn't pay the bills, he'd trained as a locksmith. Asa eventually set up on his own company, Oluso Locks, made his fortune inventing an unpickable keyless lock, then returned to his first love, painting. He'd had a wife, children and even grandchildren along the way, but had been a widower for many years. Asa was a man with boundless energy though his placid exterior usually belied that fact.

May thoroughly enjoyed their time together. They would visit exhibitions, walk the dogs in Greenwich Park, and try new restaurants in town. She would never forget the first time Asa had stayed overnight at Greenway. Fletcher entered the kitchen the following morning to find them sipping coffee at the table, Asa wrapped in May's dressing gown, both of them still muzzy with sleep. Or lack of it.

The look on Fletcher's face almost made up for May's years of sexual frustration in her marriage.

To give him credit, Fletcher had maintained a dignified silence, making polite small talk until Asa had gone upstairs to shower. As soon as the kitchen door shut behind him, Fletcher leant across the table, grinning from ear to ear. 'So, Ms Morrigan. How was it?' He waggled his eyebrows suggestively.

'Whatever do you mean?' May said. 'Your forehead seems to be going into spasms. You might want to see a doctor about that.'

Fletcher narrowed his eyes. 'You're not holding out on me, May Morrigan. I don't need *all* the details, just the headlines. Are you a happy woman this morning?'

May tried not to smile but failed miserably. She took a slow sip of coffee, making Fletcher wait that little bit longer, then set the mug down before replying with a sigh. 'It was an absolute revelation. I'd forgotten how utterly delightful sex can be.'

Fletcher bellowed with laughter. 'I'm so pleased for you!'

'It was marvellous,' she continued, feeling her face warm in remembrance.

'I haven't seen that cat-that-got-the-cream look on your face for such a long time. Does this mean things are getting serious?' He waggled his eyebrows up and down again.

'Stop it.' May swatted at him but continued to smile. 'I'm not sure I want things to get *serious*.'

'May Morrigan, you old slapper,' Fletcher said with a wink. 'I like this version of you.' He held up his mug in a toast.

May raised her mug in salute, took a sip to seal the deal, then stood to place it in the sink. 'In fact, I think I'll go join Asa in the shower.'

Fletcher chuckled and did a little dance in his seat as May regally exited the kitchen.

Asa was such a kind, attentive man. Most of the time. Then there were the moments when May wouldn't hear from him for days. She didn't mind the space. In fact, it was important to have plenty of time to herself. It was the abruptness of his disappearances that unsettled her. They would be ticking along, texting if not seeing each other most days, when suddenly he would cancel their plans and go silent.

May had asked him about it, but he'd just said that he needed time alone. Afterwards, he'd re-engage and carry on as usual. Until the next time. She'd realised that when they *were* together, May was often on edge, looking for signs that he was about to disappear again. It was becoming a problem.

'Hi-ho, May! Mind if I have a quick word?' It was May's neighbour, Geoffrey Crichton, the young MP, known in Greenway as The Cretin.

'Hello, Geoffrey,' May said.

The Cretin was wearing faded red cords, a long waxed jacket, and a bright-pink paper crown. His cheeks were ruddy, his mouth wet.

'Have you come from a Christmas lunch?' she asked, nodding at the crown stuck to his forehead with sweat. 'Or have you been inducted into a flamboyant yet impoverished royal family?'

Geoffrey looked confused, then swiped the crown from his head, crumpled it and shoved it in his coat pocket. The pink tissue paper left a residual mark across his forehead, like a nasty sunburn. 'Ah, yes. Rather boozy lunch with the Countryside Alliance people. Lot of concerns about the blight of those ruddy solar farms popping up all over the shop. Bit tight, I'm afraid.' He belched into his chest, sniggered like a naughty schoolboy, then stood staring at May.

'You wanted a word,' she prompted.

The Cretin jerked back into life. 'Yes, yes, yes… ah, yes, that's it. I'm off to see Ma and Pa for the holidays. Wondered if you might water the plants, keep an eye on the place while I'm away?'

May perked up. 'Yes, delighted to help,' she said.

'Jolly good. You've got the keys and the code for the alarm. Just make sure no one gets up to any mischief in my absence.' He nodded at May before turning back towards his house, taking a few steps, then pivoting to walk in the opposite direction towards the village, raising a hand as he passed.

May continued home with a spring in her step. Approved access to The Cretin's house. May Morrigan was going to get up to plenty of mischief indeed.

CHAPTER 7

WONDERFUL CHRISTMASTIME

Walking home hours later in the dark, Fletcher was still seething over his conversation with Clark Wolfe. They'd managed to wrap up the rehearsal just as the first little darlings arrived with harried mothers toting bags full of costumes and snacks. The ballet instructor was already barking directions as the Players left, mistaking the dusty village theatre for Sadler's Wells and the tiny toddlers for prima ballerinas.

Fletcher passed the bookshop. It was warm and glowing in the early winter darkness, but he was in no mood for company. The heath was bitterly cold, his breath expelled in indignant puffs of condensation as he mentally sifted through his altercation with Clark. Fletcher had gently suggested that Clark was perhaps showing a bit too much attention to the young Louella. He didn't want anyone to get the wrong idea, did he?

Clark had immediately flared into indignation. 'What are you suggesting? That I'm some kind of paedophile?' he said. 'Louella is an adult. If anything, *she's* been all over *me*. I'm just doing the poor girl a favour by trying to let her down gently.'

'She's barely twenty years old,' Fletcher hissed in reply. 'Up until a few months ago, she was still a teenager.' God, Clark was disgusting. The man was seventy, if he was a day. Old enough to be Louella's grandfather. 'She may be a bit starry-eyed, but I'm sure there's nothing in it on her side. Just back off, Clark. I'm warning you.'

Clark looked amused. 'Warning me? And what are you going to do if I don't back off?' He smirked, stepping closer and lowering his voice. 'I'll tell you exactly what you're going to do, old boy. Nothing. Nothing at all.' He grinned, baring his weirdly perfect teeth. '"I fart in your general direction!" Oh, Louella!' he called over his shoulder whilst keeping his eyes on Fletcher. 'Could we run through that last scene together, please?'

'Sure thing!' she replied, skipping over to join them. She looked from one man to the other, sensing the tension between them. 'Is something wrong?'

'No,' Clark said, turning to look at her. 'Everything is just peachy keen.'

It had taken all of Fletcher's self-control to remain calm and continue the rehearsal. It was the thought of speaking to May that consoled him and kept him going. Clark was the perfect candidate for May Morrigan's personal brand of justice. Perhaps they could poison him with something truly horrible. Knowing May, she would be cultivating the very thing in her garden that would do the trick beautifully. Nothing too quick though, the more suffering, the better. Clark deserved it.

Fletcher's phone buzzed in his pocket. It was Sparks trying to video call. Fletcher smoothed his hair before tapping the screen and holding the phone high to avoid the dreaded double chin.

'Hello, darling,' he said to the jerky image. There was Sparks, looking relaxed and cheerful in stark contrast to Fletcher's sullen mood.

Sparks leant in closer to the camera. 'What's happened?' he said. 'You look nonplussed. Is it that nasty Clark Wolfe ruffling your handsome feathers?'

On the screen Fletcher noticed that a man with a thick moustache had stopped on the path behind him. He seemed to be earwigging their private conversation. Fletcher moved off across the grass. He smiled at Sparks, his shoulders relaxing, his mood shifting decidedly upwards. Sparks often had that effect on him. 'Yes, who else,' he said. 'Nothing I can't handle though. How are you?'

Sparks smiled. Something in Fletcher's lower belly fluttered. 'I'm fine,' Sparks said. 'Eating far too much sambar vada. Absolutely everything here seems to be deep-fried. I had the most delicious cardamom kulfi at the beach. We must make some next summer. And the dosas! I could live on the dosas alone.' Sparks was bubbling over with enthusiasm. The Chennai sun had deepened the colour of his skin, throwing his white beard and bright golden eyes into contrast. Fletcher could almost feel the warmth radiating from the small screen. He ached with longing to be snuggling into Sparks's broad chest, preferably in a big bed under a heavy duvet.

Sparks's voice had ground to a halt. His eyes softened, seeming to read Fletcher's mind. 'You look cold,' he said. 'Go home. We'll talk tomorrow.' A young child jumped on Sparks's back, squealing with glee. 'Addy, you should be in bed,' Sparks said. 'Off you go. Remember, Father Christmas is watching.' The child jumped down and ran out of the room.

Fletcher had almost forgotten he was standing in the middle of the heath. The cold wind cut through his wool coat, sharply reminding him. 'I miss you,' he said. 'You would make a very sexy Father Christmas.'

'Would you like to sit on my knee and tell me exactly what you want for Christmas?' Sparks winked.

Fletcher chuckled, feeling a twitch in his trousers. 'More than anything.'

．　．　．

Fletcher opened Greenway's front door to the sound of May and Minty shouting in the library.

'I'm just asking you to please not bring your phone into the library,' May was saying. 'It's a technology-free area.'

'That's a stupid rule,' Minty replied. 'It's the twenty-first century, dear.'

He stopped in the entry hall, realising they hadn't heard him come in. He and Sparks had spent a few minutes debating which of them would look sexiest in a red velvet Santa costume before hinting at what they'd like to stuff in each other's Christmas stockings. Fletcher wanted to get upstairs, quickly knock one out, then have a lie down before dinner. He was making Nigella's gammon cooked in Coca-Cola as a test run for the Christmas Eve meal. It had been simmering in the slow cooker all day, scenting the house with its sweet and savoury aroma.

Could he make it to his room without being heard? He slipped off his shoes and tiptoed towards the stairs.

'Fletcher?! Is that you?' May opened the door to the library.

Fletcher froze in his tracks. *Damn it.*

'Yes,' he said. 'I was just going to have a little lie down. Exhausting rehearsal today.' As he said it, Fletcher realised he felt very tired indeed.

May stepped into the hall, shutting the library door behind her with a bang. She looked a bit peaky herself. 'Minty is driving me round the bend. I think she's bored. Most of her friends have gone to stay with their children or grandchildren for the holidays. Cass is no use at all. She's either out running, making some disgusting "food", or hiding in her room. Minty has no one to play with. Do you think Desi would be up for a playdate, so to speak?'

Fletcher thought it over. 'Why don't you send Minty to the rehearsal tomorrow? She and Desi can go for coffee, or I'll find something for her to do. That'll occupy her for an afternoon at least.'

'You're a saint, Fletcher Redmond.' May kissed him on the cheek. 'What would I do without you?'

CHAPTER 8

THANK GOD IT'S CHRISTMAS

It was 1964. May and Minty were shouting at each other downstairs as usual. A door slammed. A door opened. The voices continued. Cass was young and blooming, her whole life a great mystery spooling out ahead of her. Even the day in front of her was a great unknown.

Then life and the world went into fast forward and Cass realised with a jolt that she was sixty-nine. She wasn't a young girl anymore. Her body felt cumbersome and aching in the strange bed. She was waking up from another heavy nap, in what was now her sister's home. It was a house that was familiar yet foreign. So many years had passed since she was last at Greenway. That gulf of time weighed heavily on Cass.

She continued to lie, aware of her heart gently thumping in her chest as memories flitted across her consciousness. Faces, laughter, sunshine, music. Always music. Then darkness, pain, fear. A small hand in hers. Those thoughts were best avoided.

So much work, travel, busyness. Faceless people in and out of her life. Things that had seemed so important at the time, she could barely remember now. What did any of that matter? What difference had it made to anyone? Then harsh fluorescent lights overhead, poking and prodding, more fear, more pain. And now here, back in this house, hiding in her room once again, listening to the same angry voices from below. Cass had come full circle. The emotional vertigo was staggering. What had been the bloody point of it all?

She would have to tell May soon. There were too many secrets between them. The longer she left it, the harder it would be.

Cass turned her face to the wall. She closed her eyes and thought again of the hand that had all too briefly held on to hers.

CHAPTER 9

SILENT NIGHT

May watched Cass chomp through her bowl of broccoli and quinoa, sipping another green juice, while the rest of them enjoyed Fletcher's delicious ham with mashed potatoes and a fruity Valpolicella. The dogs lay under the table, ready in case someone happened to drop a plate of meat. May took another bite and wondered what had happened to the exuberant, over-the-top sister she remembered.

The last time she'd seen Cass had been over ten years before. Cass had been promoting a new nightclub on Mykonos and May had flown over for a long weekend. They'd drunk far too much sambuca and mastiha, danced until the wee hours, ate gyros at 3am, then had a screaming argument about which one of them had lost the key to their accommodation. After climbing through a window, knocking over a table in the process, they'd reconciled in the tiny kitchen over baklava purchased from the bakery that was opening as they'd stumbled home. May couldn't imagine the woman in front of her doing any of those things.

Sitting at the table without make-up, Cass looked pinched and pale. The restricted diet and constant exercise hadn't improved her energy levels either. She seemed to be either exercising or sleeping.

Of course, Cass had never done things by halves. Her love affairs, her career, the drinking, the partying had been all-consuming for as long as May could remember. Perhaps this new obsession with health was another side of the same compulsiveness. While May accepted, even enjoyed growing older, Cass seemed to be fighting it tooth and nail. And the boobs were definitely new.

'A friend is coming over later,' May said. 'We're going to have a drink in the library. You should join us.' She looked at Cass. 'I think you'll like Bastian.'

The library was looking especially lovely as May stirred a jug of Advocaat and lemonade. A bowl of ice and maraschino cherries sat ready to garnish their snowballs. It was May's favourite festive drink. There was something so jolly about a bright-red cherry.

A wedge of Stilton rested on a platter with sticks of celery, sliced pears and a selection of crackers. May purchased a wheel of the English cheese every December from Neal's Yard Dairy and they nibbled their way through it over the holiday period. Like champagne, the salty blue cheese could only be called Stilton if it was produced in certain areas of England. In May's opinion, the Neal's Yard Stilton was the best. It was a delicious annual treat.

She was adding bowls of Twiglets and minty Matchmakers to the low table in the centre of the room when Fletcher came in. He was wearing a red tartan sweater vest, sparkly earrings with red nails and was looking very festive.

'Don't you look handsome,' May said.

He touched the earrings. 'Not too much?'

'Of course not.' She kissed him on the cheek. 'Come and have a snowball.'

Minty toddled in as May was making the drinks. 'Did I hear the delicious clink of ice? Oooh, snowballs. How lovely. Two cherries please.'

Bastian arrived soon afterwards carrying an amaryllis bulb in a pretty pot. 'Something for your desk,' he said, handing it to May. 'I love an amaryllis, one of the few flowers that bloom in winter when we desperately need a reminder that spring is coming.'

Sebastian Lovelace had managed May's bookshop, Burgos Books, for years. He was an affable polymath, an ardent lover, an avid reader, and happened to be four and a half feet tall. He'd met May during the most difficult period of her life, when she was nursing her husband through cancer, and had become a treasured and trusted friend. Fletcher adored him, Minty had a crush on him and the dogs knew that Bastian carried treats in his pockets especially for them.

They were settling down with drinks and snacks when Cass wandered in still wearing her yoga trousers, which seemed to be her uniform of choice. 'Hello,' she said, extending a hand towards Bastian. 'I'm Cass.' Bastian paused, looking from May to Cass. 'Didn't May tell you we're twins?'

'It didn't come up,' he said with a smile. 'Two of you. How extraordinary.'

'That's one way of putting it,' Minty said. 'They've been a handful since the day they were born. Couldn't get out into the world fast enough, either one of them. The birth was like a bloody log flume with one baby after another dropping out of me.'

May grimaced at Minty's choice of words then turned to Bastian. 'Have you heard anything about the stabbing this morning?'

'Nancy Drew, on the case,' Cass retorted, making a drink at the trolley.

'Ignore her,' May said.

Bastian smiled at both sisters before replying. 'Harold and the family were informed. Jocasta is in a bad way, of course. It's such a shocking thing to happen.'

'Who found him?' Fletcher asked.

The dachshunds had chomped through their treats from Bastian then burrowed under their blanket beside the fire.

'Evie Barr,' Bastian replied. 'She was out at sunrise, as usual, and found Caspar collapsed in the circle. Unfortunately, he was already dead.'

'Ah yes, the crow lady,' May said.

'Crow lady? Blackheath gets more and more bonkers every year,' Cass said, taking a seat with the others. Her "cocktail" consisted of sparkling water, ice, and a slice of lemon.

May had mixed feelings about Cass being there. On the one hand, it was good that Cass was out of her room for once. On the other, May wished that she would just sod off.

'Evie feeds the crows every morning,' May explained. 'It's quite a sight. They recognise her and start gathering around as soon as she steps onto the heath.'

'You have to be up at the crack of dawn for the pleasure though,' Fletcher said. Early mornings were never his thing.

'If Evie found him and he was already dead, that means that when he was stabbed it was still dark. She's always there just as the sun is coming up,' May said. There were lights on the heath paths, but at that time on a winter morning it would be almost deserted. Though the Millennium Circle was exposed in daylight, in the dark there would be relative privacy.

Good Lord, the dogs had started farting beside the fire. The smell was appalling. They'd had far too many treats because of the holidays. Fletcher was wafting a hand around. Thankfully,

Minty had dozed off in her chair or she would've commented on it, loudly.

May removed a tipping glass from Minty's hand and sat it on the table. 'I wasn't finished with that,' she mumbled before drifting off again.

'Maybe the detective is right,' May continued, 'and it's just a local hoodlum who attempted to mug Caspar.' She shrugged.

'If I didn't know better,' Cass said with a grin, 'I'd think you were disappointed.'

CHAPTER 10

STEP INTO CHRISTMAS

Fletcher was attempting to follow the conversation about the murder, but his mind was on other things: the damn panto and the lovely Sparks.

The panto was coming together at last. Desi was working miracles on the costumes with their meagre budget. She and Fletcher had raided the storage facility where she kept her past projects, bolts of fabric, bits of trimming, various sewing machines, a library of clothing patterns, boxes of fabric dye, and buckets of buttons. Fletcher had spotted a stack of boxes at the back labelled *Dido*, Desi's daughter who'd died when she was still a young woman. Desi never spoke about her. Losing a child must be unbearably painful regardless of age. He wondered how Caspar's parents were coping.

'Are Caspar's parents local?' he asked.

'No,' May said. 'I don't think so. I've certainly never met them. Do you know, Bastian?'

Bastian shook his head. 'I've only chatted with Caspar when he came into the shop with Tansy. He didn't grow up in Black-heath, I know that. I think it was somewhere on the South Coast.'

'I can't imagine what they must be feeling right now, losing a child like that,' Fletcher said.

'Can I make anyone a drink?' Cass jumped up and moved over to the trolley. Her own glass was still almost full. Fletcher noticed that Bastian was giving her an odd look. What did that mean? Surely, he wasn't attracted to her. Cass was a lovely woman, but she was decades older than Bastian.

That reminded Fletcher of his conversation with Clark about Louella. Clark was fifty years older than Louella. Fletcher was no prude, he just couldn't help feeling protective. Nothing untoward had happened yet, but he could tell that the intent was there on Clark's behalf. The man had a dreadful reputation with women, particularly young ones. Of course, Louella was an adult, but she still seemed so fresh and innocent. Which was probably why Clark was targeting her.

Malin Tanzer, their Wendy, was just as lovely as Louella, but Malin was a bit older and wiser. She wasn't charmed by Clark's cheap charisma or giddy over the fact that he'd been on TV and in a few films. Malin could spot the sleaze under the sparkle. She could hold her own when it came to Clark Wolfe.

The same couldn't be said for Fletcher's Peter Pan. He was being played by a young local dad, Oliver Harden, who'd done a bit of theatre as a teen. Oliver's performance was solid but he needed a bit more oomph. Of course, it was impossible to see anyone else when Clark was onstage flouncing around, hogging the limelight. He'd been particularly overbearing that morning, interrupting other actors, ad-libbing lines, chewing the scenery at every opportunity. Fletcher would have a word with Oliver about how he could hold his own when sharing the stage with Clark's Widow Twankey.

'Fletcher? Did you hear me?' May was speaking to him.

'Apologies,' he said. 'I was miles away. Say it again.'

'I was suggesting that we go see Harold tomorrow. Would you like to come? Perhaps bake something to take?'

Fletcher would love to bake something for Harold. There was a recipe for an almond cake that he'd been planning to try. When would he have the time? The bloody panto had taken over his life.

'I won't have a chance to bake anything,' he said with regret. 'I'll pick up some good bread, fruit and cheese in the village and come with you, if you go in the afternoon. I've got never-ending rehearsals in Neverland first thing.'

'That's perfect,' May said. 'They're probably more in need of real sustenance rather than cakes anyway.'

Poor Harold. He'd raised his daughter, Jocasta, on his own after her mother had left them for a Spanish waiter and moved to Ibiza. Harold and Jocasta were very close. In fact, May had said there was concern at one point that Jocasta would never have a life of her own, she was so dedicated to her father. Then, in her forties, she'd met Caspar through mutual friends. Being that bit older, they'd wasted no time. Jocasta and Caspar married and had sweet Tansy within a year. The three of them plus Harold formed a tight family unit.

How was Sparks getting on with his own family in Chennai? Fletcher envied him the big, mad, extended clan. Fletcher's own family weren't very close, marked by generations of dysfunction. It was a part of his life he'd learnt to accept after years of therapy, but it still made him sad. Every time he and Sparks had managed to chat there were smiling faces in the background popping in to say hello, children whooping with delight, running to the camera to show Fletcher a new drawing or an insect they'd captured.

He did a quick calculation. It would be almost four in the morning there. Sparks would be fast asleep. Fletcher could imagine him on his side, knees pulled up, the perfect big spoon. He even missed Sparks's gurgling snore that could reach shocking levels. More than once he'd worried that the sound of it would wake May across the landing.

Christ on a bike, what was that dreadful odour? The ruddy dogs again. George's canine IBS was getting worse.

Fletcher realised that the party in the library was breaking up. May had started gathering glasses, plates, and bowls then placing them on the trolley to be wheeled back to the kitchen. Fletcher helped her as Minty continued to snore in her chair. Bastian led Cass to a corner of the library, ostensibly to admire the Christmas tree, but their faces looked surprisingly serious. They whispered together for a moment before Bastian said goodnight. Afterwards, Cass seemed thoughtful and distracted, silently sitting at the kitchen table as they washed up and prepared to go upstairs to bed. She didn't even make her usual bedtime green juice.

What was Bastian up to now?

CHAPTER 11

CHRISTMAS BLUES

After putting the kitchen to rights, May texted Asa to confirm their plans for the following evening. He was usually up late, painting, the studio hazy from the Plasencia cigars he only smoked at the easel. Once the work was on display, if one got close enough it was possible to catch their earthy scent imbued in the canvases. Sometimes when she was staying over, he would get up in the night to work then come back to bed in the wee hours smelling of paint, turpentine and cedary smoke. It was better than any aphrodisiac.

Asa responded in the affirmative, they were still on for dinner. May felt relief, then chided herself for caring so much. Asa was a decent man, but in her heart she knew he was never going to be the love of her life. To remind herself of this, she kept a list in one of her ledgers of the ways in which he irritated or disappointed her:

> *– The way he sometimes speaks about women, commenting on their appearance or boasting about other women he's dated.*
> *Insecure.*
> *– Changes plans at the last minute. Unreliable.*

– Being late, sometimes very late, without texting to let me know. Inconsiderate.

– Books he claims to love but has obviously never read, his opinions on art that drift into bitterness. Pretentious.

But he was warm and enthusiastic when they were together. He made her laugh and had reawakened a part of her that she'd thought was long dead. Namely, her libido. The fact was, she liked Asa Oluso and that was enough for now.

Upstairs, as she washed her face and brushed her teeth, May wondered if she'd ever been in a healthy relationship. Her family relationships were a shitshow, though not without love. The passions of her youth had been fun, fiery, and fulfilling, but one couldn't really call them healthy. Those relationships had been all about hunger and excitement, trying to complete herself with another human being. To give him some credit, James had been nothing like that. His apathy had given May space to become whole on her own. James had never been interested in knowing May, not really. Not down to her bones. He'd barely skimmed the surface in their forty years together.

At best, James had been someone to come home to, another sentient being in the house. What May had taken as stability, had been indifference. What she'd thought was care, had been control. She'd come to realise that her marriage had been an illusion. While she'd been honest and committed to James, he'd been doing whatever the fuck he pleased behind her back.

May Morrigan had never met her equal. Apart from Fletcher. She realised that she'd loved Fletcher Redmond longer than she'd loved anyone else. He knew all her darkest secrets, and loved her still. They'd had their disagreements, but they both valued the friendship enough to work at repairing it and had come out closer in the end. Perhaps she *had* managed to have at least one healthy relationship after all.

She and Fletcher would visit Harold Lambert the following

day and pay their respects. Harold and Jocasta were lovely people. Part of an old Blackheath family, May had known Harold her whole life. They were never particularly close, but they'd run in the same circles as children. Childhood friendships, the people who had known you before you were moulded by life and the bigger world, remained some of the strongest and most valued as one grew older. It was a shame they were caught up in such a tragedy, and so close to the holidays too. Christmas would never be the same for them.

Had Caspar been so lovely? May hadn't known him well at all. He seemed like a kind, adoring father. Surely, Jocasta wouldn't be attracted to anything less. But one never knew. Perhaps there were skeletons in Caspar's closet, ones of which even the Lamberts were unaware. If there were, May would find out. She'd start with a little chat with Harold.

Then in the evening, Asa. They'd go out for a nice meal, admire the Christmas lights in the village, then wander back to his house, a Victorian that he was constantly "doing up". The floorboards were half sanded, the walls half plastered. The kitchen was made up of various mismatched free-standing cabinets, with a hole in the ceiling that would one day house the chimney for a wood-burning stove. Not a single project in the whole house was complete, but the armchairs were comfy, the table was clean and the bed was enormous. May couldn't wait.

But before all of that, she'd speak to Evie, the crow lady. Maybe she'd seen something that seemed unimportant at the time. May set an alarm just in case. The best way to find Evie Barr was to be on the heath at dawn.

CHAPTER 12

DO THEY KNOW IT'S CHRISTMAS?

*W*ho was this Sebastian Lovelace and what did he know?

Cass lay on her bed, pondering this question. He seemed charming and kind then; at the first opportunity he'd drawn her away from the others, gently insisting that she visit him at the bookshop the following day. He'd said nothing else. No explanation. How bizarre.

Why had this peculiar, but harmless behaviour chilled Cass to the bone?

Bastian had a way of looking that was slightly unsettling. It reminded her of May's dogs, always sniffing at every little thing on their walks. Cass imagined their tiny minds running through assessments and calculations: *urine... canine... elderly dog... grain-free diet.* Or perhaps: *chicken bone... free-range... deep-fried... eaten by someone with chronic halitosis.*

Bastian was like that. He didn't just look at a person, he assessed them. He'd assessed Cass and seen something that made him want to speak to her in private. What secret had he divined? Lord knew, she had plenty of them.

Cass often thought that her life would make a great Netflix

series, if she could just find the energy to sit down and write it. Born firmly English middle-class, she'd dropped out of Cambridge to travel across the US one summer and never left, following Led Zeppelin on their North American tour. Friends with the band, she'd photographed the boys behind the scenes, then sold the images to magazines all over the world. Soon she was travelling with other bands, creating images for album covers and writing articles about her experiences. Then she'd turned her camera on the fans, capturing the raucous energy, the tears, the joy and the violence that so often surrounded stardom. Her photographs defined the rock music era of the 1970s. What haunted Cass were the images that were never published. The ones that existed only in her memory.

The drink, the drugs, the groupies grasping for their shot at fame. The flipside to the glamour and glitz was a great deal of tragedy. Young lives cut short. Talent wasted. People used and abused, then discarded when their light stopped shining so brightly. It was an unforgiving business.

Cass had remained on the edges of the chaos for the most part. She'd had her fair share of fun, but had done her best to keep a healthy distance from the worst aspects of the culture. She'd been an observer. Watching, documenting, learning from the mistakes of others. Eventually, her focus had shifted to the women of rock and their personal struggles to be heard and respected. In that community of creative women, Cass had found her people. She started writing and her biographies of Sandie Shaw, Dusty Springfield and Kiki Dee had become bestsellers. Funny that she, May and Fletcher had each ended up with lives centred around books in one way or another.

Lying in bed in her childhood home, the photographs, the books all felt like they belonged to a different person. It was as if her whole life had been a dream and she'd just woken up in Greenway to live it all over again. Was she stuck in the past now or could she return to that other life? Did she want to?

Cass sighed. She would go see Bastian the following day, see what he had to say. It was almost exciting, the prospect of a little intrigue.

She realised she'd forgotten to drink her evening green juice. Did it really matter? Cass decided that it probably didn't make a blind bit of difference.

CHAPTER 13

O, LITTLE TOWN OF BETHLEHEM

May tried to silently put on her coat and boots in the entryway without waking Minty, who operated on MMT (Minty Mean Time), which meant sleeping and waking whenever she damn well pleased.

It was still dark outside, the dachshunds were confused but excited about the earlier than usual walk. May slipped on their jumpers, harnesses and leads before opening the door.

Even though it was technically morning, the heath was in complete darkness. Sunrise wasn't until 8am. May had fifteen minutes to walk the dogs, let them do their business, then get them back into the house before Evie appeared to feed the crows. Two energetic dachshunds and a murder of crows would not make an ideal combination.

She wandered out to the centre of the grass, letting the dogs off their leads. 'Be quick,' she whispered, though there was no one around to hear. May turned in a slow circle, making certain she was alone. Eyes seemed to prickle the back of her neck. But she was being silly, there was no one else out yet. She turned back to the dogs.

Evelyn Barr had been feeding the crows on Blackheath every

morning for years. Before Evie, her husband Marty was seen at dawn each day, a mob of crows surrounding him, all jogging for position. Marty died from cancer around the same time that James recovered from his illness then left May for the woman he'd been seeing for decades. In that first year, when she could barely sleep, May would watch Evie from her bedroom window as the sun came up, two women united in grief though separated by oceans of circumstance. While May had lost a husband, Evie had lost the love of her life.

If she was being completely honest, a small part of May envied Evie. Marty Barr had died still loving Evie with all his heart. If fate was fair, then Marty would still be alive and James would be the one whose ashes were sprinkled under the trees in Greenwich Park. Unfortunately, fate was a cruel bastard.

Marty was gone, but his love remained. Evie communed with him every morning by feeding the crows. As May had watched from her window, she imagined that love surrounding Evie, holding her close and keeping her warm on the frosty mornings, taking her hand when it was time to return home.

May stood in the middle of the cold, dark heath, feeling more deeply alone than she had in months. And there was a killer about with a very sharp knife. She called the dogs and bent to snap on their leads.

'Hello, lovely.' The voice was very near.

May gasped then clutched at her chest. 'Evie, you scared the life out of me. I didn't hear you coming.'

Evie chuckled. 'Sorry. Old habits die hard.' She tapped the side of her nose. 'What brings you out this morning?' The crows had already spotted her and were beginning to gather around. Bess and George pulled against their harnesses.

'I heard you found Caspar yesterday,' May said, maintaining an iron grip on the leads. 'How are you doing?'

Evie nodded, her mouth grim. 'Poor man. Not the first time

I've had to deal with death, as you know. Still, always horrible. Have you been to see Harold?'

May shook her head. 'Not yet. Fletcher and I are going this afternoon. I was wondering, what made you go over to the Millennium Circle in the first place? You usually stay around this patch, don't you?'

Evie's place was a big flat in a converted house a few doors down from Greenway. As Marty had done, she usually stayed on the area of grass in front of their building.

'You'll think I'm mad, but it was the crows.' She gestured to the birds keeping a safe distance from the dogs, patiently waiting for their breakfast. 'I can't explain it exactly, but they were acting odd and kept hopping over in that direction. Normally, I wouldn't notice if there was a family of elephants over there, but the birds wouldn't give up.'

May knew a bit about crows. She had a stuffed trio of the birds in her library. Intriguing animals. Surprisingly intelligent. Their knowledge and distress didn't surprise her.

'Was he… already gone when you found him?' May asked. The dogs had started to whine, backing against May's feet as the crows began to circle.

Evie nodded. 'And before you ask, I didn't see anyone running away or anything like that. The police asked me all the same questions.' She shrugged. 'No idea who could've done it.'

As they were speaking, the heath woke up. The sun peeked over the horizon, spilling amber light across the frozen grass. The crows hopped about, growing impatient, as the dogs spotted a gap in the crowd and pulled May towards home. Parents and children appeared, on their way to St Julian's primary school. Dog walkers and runners traipsed along the paths. Like a film set when the director shouts 'Action!', they were suddenly surrounded by life.

May said goodbye, leaving Evie to the crows and Marty's memory. She stopped at the gate of Greenway to look back over the heath. The wintry sunlight gilded the spire of St Julian's, a child's laughter rang out. May had been born in Blackheath, in her mother's bedroom at Greenway, just a few feet from where she was standing. No doubt she would die there as well. Minty's desire to return to the village where she planned to end her days was perfectly understandable. May couldn't imagine living or dying anywhere else.

CHAPTER 14

I WISH IT COULD BE CHRISTMAS EVERY DAY

Fletcher was still pondering Bastian's intentions concerning Cass the following morning as he gathered the Players together for rehearsal.

'Let's work on the wedding scene and big finale,' he said, clapping his hands to get everyone's attention. Clark was hovering around Louella, reading the script over her shoulder, leaning in much closer than necessary while shooting catty little looks at Fletcher. The toast and coffee Fletcher had inhaled for breakfast gurgled in his stomach.

Oliver and Malin took their places as the bride and groom. Clark, playing the mother of the bride, tore himself away from Louella to reluctantly join them onstage. Peter Pan and Wendy getting married felt like sacrilege. They were children in the story, after all. But, a panto needed a big finale, if it involved a wedding, all the better. J M Barrie would just have to suck it up. To be fair, Barrie did write an epilogue saying that Wendy eventually married a Lost Boy and had a son. He just didn't say which one.

'Ready?' Cecil, the pianist and scene-painter, held his hands poised above the keys.

'Right-o,' Fletcher said. 'Off you go.' The scene kicked into motion as Fletcher took a seat next to Desi. She was sewing white lace to a length of blue flannel, Wendy's nightgown.

The cast danced and sang while Peter and Wendy made lovey eyes at each other. Then it was time for the finale where Tinkerbell flies above the wedding party.

'Louella, all set?' Fletcher asked. On her nod, he motioned to one of the stagehands who operated the rigging that lifted Tinkerbell above the rest of the cast. It was a simple stunt that provided an unexpected and surprisingly magical ending.

Louella played her part well, gracefully hovering above the rest, creating a gloriously camp tableaux. Fletcher felt something akin to pride until he noticed Clark looking up at Louella with a lascivious grin. The man was relentless.

'All right, well done, everyone,' he shouted. 'Take a quick break then we'll run through it again.' Fletcher let out a deep sigh. He would have to speak to Clark again.

'I saw it too,' Desi said. She pointed towards Clark with her needle. 'It's like watching a shark circle a mackerel with those dead eyes of his.'

'I've had a word with him once already,' Fletcher said. 'He just won't leave her alone.'

'I've known him for almost fifty years.' Desi returned to her stitching as she spoke. 'He's always been the same. Someone should castrate the old dog. I've got a big pair of scissors in my basket. You hold him down and I'll do the dirty work.'

Fletcher laughed. 'If only it were that easy.'

'Desi,' he said, eyes glued to Clark, who had his arm around Louella's shoulders. 'You remember May's mother, Minty? She seems to be at a loose end. I wondered if you might take her out for a coffee this morning. My treat.'

'I always liked Minty,' she said. 'We had some fun back in the day. I'll take her over to Dementia Gardens, introduce her around. If she's bored, there's always something happening there.'

'Thanks, Desi. You're a lifesaver,' he said. Fletcher stood up, clapping his hands together. 'Let's go back to Hook's comeuppance scene. Where's my Captain Hook?' he shouted, as Justin, a local father recently made redundant, stumbled onto the stage. Justin's beer belly wasn't really in keeping with the character as Fletcher imagined him, but he'd thrown himself into the role and seemed to be having a good time. It's what amateur dramatics was all about. 'We'll begin with the "look behind you" gag.'

The actors took their places on stage. Louella stepped forwards to address the audience. 'Has anyone seen a mean old pirate around?' She cupped her hand to one ear, waiting for the audience response.

'Look behind you!' Fletcher said with as much enthusiasm as he could muster.

'Who's the lardy-arse playing Hook?' Minty said, appearing beside Fletcher. 'Looks like he's about to give birth to triplets.'

'Minty, keep your voice down,' Fletcher hissed as the actors continued their lines.

'This came for you.' She tossed a parcel in Fletcher's direction before lowering herself onto a seat. 'What's *Eat, Drink and Be Mary*? Funny name for a shop.'

'Minty, please!' he said, stuffing the package under his chair, label-side down. 'Did you walk here on your own?'

'Don't be ridiculous.' She tried to whisper but it made her dentures slide around in her mouth. 'I took an Udder.'

'Uber,' Fletcher corrected automatically.

'Desi!' Minty had given up on whispering. 'How are you?'

Desi, bless her, immediately set the fabric aside. 'Minty, why don't we go for a little catch-up.' She helped Minty up from her seat, gave Fletcher a wink and led Minty away from the actors.

Fletcher watched the two women leave, arm-in-arm. They were giggling before they'd reached the door. Desi would keep Minty entertained for a while. Fletcher relaxed a tiny bit. Maybe it would all work out after all. Onstage, the play continued.

'Look behind you,' Fletcher said.

CHAPTER 15

BLUE CHRISTMAS

'Fletcher, do keep up.' May and Fletcher were on their way to visit Harold Lambert.

'I don't know why you insist on walking so quickly. It's not a race,' he replied, panting heavily. The Lambert family lived in a big house on the Cator Estate, a private neighbourhood on the east side of the village.

'You're not even carrying anything,' May said. She held up the basket of food she'd put together for the family. 'Honestly, Fletch. I'm going to buy you a treadmill.'

'You'll do no such thing!' he said, horrified at the thought. 'If I want to walk, I've got Greenwich Park and the whole heath at my feet. I don't need some ridiculous machine cluttering up the place.' He bumped into May's back when she stopped abruptly in front of the Lambert home.

'We're here,' she said.

'Yes, I see that,' he replied, straightening his coat and taking deep breaths.

May waited until his breathing settled. 'Shall we, Grandad?' she said, offering her arm.

Fletcher swiped it away. 'Silly woman,' he said, causing May to laugh. 'Grandad, my arse.' He took the basket from May, held his head high and marched towards the front door.

'It's not beyond the realms of possibility for a seventy-year-old man to be a grandfather,' May said as she followed him up the path.

'Grandfathers are stuffy, boring old things. Besides, in order to be a grandfather, one must first be a father, which involves doing something with a woman which I've never done.' He knocked on the door.

'Not never,' May said with a smirk. 'I think Pamela Clarendon would have something to say about that.'

Fletcher exhaled loudly. 'That was at uni. I was young and confused. Besides, everyone experiments at uni. If I remember correctly, Pamela Clarendon also spent some time in your–'

Jocasta opened the door, her eyes pink and puffy, mercifully silencing Fletcher. She welcomed them inside. 'Dad's in the kitchen,' she said. 'Do come through and I'll put the kettle on. I sent Tansy to nursery, thought it was best to stick to her usual schedule. Better to be there where things are normal and jolly.' She spoke over her shoulder as they followed her through the house. May noticed that Jocasta's dress was on inside out, the white tag bobbing under her ponytail as she walked.

Harold Lambert sat at the head of a long table in the enormous kitchen, staring into space. He was dressed as if for the office, though he'd retired from banking years before. There was an awkward moment before Harold became aware of their arrival, then his gentility snapped to attention and he stood to greet them, extending his hand. 'May. Fletcher. So kind of you to come.'

Fletcher handed the basket to Jocasta. 'We brought a few things for you, just to keep you going.'

Harold nodded and sat down again. 'So kind of you.'

'Do sit,' Jocasta said. 'I'll put the kettle on. Tansy's at nursery. We thought it best if she sticks to her usual schedule.'

It was like listening to a record on repeat. Grief had turned them into robots.

'We won't stay long,' May said. 'We just wanted to express our sympathy and see if there's anything we can do for you.'

'So kind,' Harold replied.

'Jo, come sit down. I'll do that.' Fletcher ushered Jocasta to a chair at the table before going to prepare the tea.

May turned and took her hand, then looked her in the eye. 'How are you coping, dear?'

Jocasta looked down at her lap, but held tight to May. 'As well as can be expected. Tansy doesn't understand, of course. She keeps asking for Caspar. I sent her to nursery today. Best to keep to her...' Her voice trailed away. 'I already said that, didn't I?' She looked up at May, her eyes full of tears. 'I just can't believe it. My head keeps insisting that it's impossible. He can't be gone. It's too absurd.'

May nodded. 'It *is* absurd. It's completely illogical.' She squeezed Jocasta's hand. 'Your head will catch up eventually. Just be kind to yourself and don't try to do too much. Grief will have its way with you, one way or another. Best not to fight it. It only prolongs the agony.'

Harold cleared his throat and coughed, then swiped at his eyes with a large white handkerchief. 'He shouldn't have been out at that hour. Not safe anymore. Even for a fit young man. Don't know what the world is coming to.'

Fletcher set mugs of tea in front of each of them then took the seat opposite May. With Harold in his suit and tie at the head of the table, it felt as if they were attending a board meeting. Perhaps that was the environment in which Harold felt most in control. Grief had its formidable grip on him as well.

'Did he often go for a run in the morning?' May asked.

Jocasta shook her head. 'He usually runs... *ran* after work. Said it cleared his head. For some reason, he decided to go out early yesterday. Tansy had been up in the night. I was so tired, I didn't even hear him get up.'

'Was he stressed at work? I've heard running is good for dealing with stress?' May said.

Jocasta shook her head again. 'Not particularly. Work is always a bit stressful. Fundraising is never-ending, but things have been running quite smoothly lately. Christmas puts people in the giving spirit.'

Caspar had founded a charity that offered free tutoring for disadvantaged young people.

'He was a very generous man,' Fletcher said. 'How are his folks doing? Must've been a horrible shock.'

Jocasta looked up with surprise. 'Caspar didn't have parents. Well, of course he did, but he never knew them. He grew up in care, worked hard to go to university. That's why he started the charity, to help young people like himself.'

'I didn't realise that,' May said, sitting up at this new information. 'Bastian said Caspar grew up on the coast?'

'Yes.' Jocasta sipped her tea, a sad smile flickering across her face. 'It's quite a romantic story, actually. He was left on the steps of The Chapel in Broadstairs just before Christmas. In a basket, no less. Like Moses.' The smile grew wider. It seemed to be a favourite story. 'He grew up on the South Coast. We met when he came to London to seek his fortune, like Dick Whittington, minus the cat.' As she finished speaking, her smile slipped away, replaced once again by sadness.

'Did he ever try to find his parents?' May asked.

Jocasta sighed. 'Yes, he was always trying. It was a… a point of tension between us. I'm afraid I wasn't very understanding. He had *us*. Why did he need to find someone who'd deserted him as a baby?'

'He never found them?' Fletcher asked.

'No, he had so little to go on. The church gave him the blanket he was wrapped in, but the basket is long gone. His mother, or whoever had left him there, had put a photograph in with him, but it was just of a pair of hands, no faces. Not much use.'

'A pair of hands? How odd,' May said. 'I wonder, would it be possible to see it?'

Jocasta stood up, grateful to be doing something useful. 'Yes, it's in the bedroom. Caspar liked to keep it close.' She went off to find it.

'He was a good lad,' Harold said. 'But quite obsessed with finding his family. Jocasta found it difficult, thought we should be enough. But, she's had me her whole life. It's hard to understand what it must've been like for him, not knowing where he came from.'

Harold Lambert certainly knew where he came from: a long line of English bankers. May would guess that somewhere in that Tardis of a house was a framed family tree going back centuries.

Jocasta returned, pink-cheeked from rushing up and down the stairs. She handed the photograph to May and placed what looked like a pile of rags on the table. 'This is the blanket he was wrapped in,' she said. 'It looks handmade. They must've been very poor.'

May looked at the photograph while Fletcher unfolded the blanket. It was a colour photo of two hands, one grasping the other, on what looked like a wooden bench. One hand was slim and feminine, the other broad and masculine.

'He always assumed they were the hands of his mother and father, though I suppose that isn't necessarily the case,' Jocasta said.

'She's wearing a distinctive ring,' May said, showing the image to Fletcher.

'It's a Claddagh ring,' Jocasta said. 'An Irish wedding ring. At least it seems his parents were married, perhaps just too poor to raise a child.'

'My sister had a ring like that when we were younger,' May said. 'They were fashionable at the time, so not necessarily worn as a wedding ring. The pose seems to be mimicking the hands on the ring.'

Fletcher looked at the photo. May was right. The hands were grasped together in the very same way.

'And there's something written on the back,' she said, turning it over.

Caspar, all my love is yours. It belongs to you and with you it will remain, though fate exiles the rest of me from you forever.

'Written to the baby or the father?' May asked, turning the photo over again. 'The handwriting looks feminine, maybe his mother's, but the language is awfully flowery for the late-twentieth century.'

Jocasta took the photograph and looked at it as if for the first time. 'The vicar assumed it was written to the baby. That's why they christened him Caspar. Campbell was the surname of his first foster family. He was with them just a few weeks, but the name stuck. I wish I'd been more supportive of his search. It was so important to him.' She began to cry again. 'He'd even done one of those ancestry DNA tests online, hoping to find a connection to someone somewhere.'

'Now, now.' Harold clumsily patted her hand, offering what comfort he could.

'Would you mind if I photographed these?' May asked. 'That probably sounds odd, but I know someone who's very good at this sort of thing. Perhaps you can finally fulfil this wish for Caspar.'

Jocasta eagerly handed back the photo then wiped her face on her sleeve. 'Do you really think so?'

'We can but try,' May said as she used her phone to snap images of both the photograph and the blanket.

They took their leave of Harold and Jocasta soon after,

drawing in deep breaths of cold air once they were outside to wash the sadness from their lungs.

'Let's go see Bastian,' May said. 'He'll know where to go from here.'

'Do you really think Caspar's parentage had anything to do with his death?' Fletcher asked, huffing and puffing as he tried to keep up with her.

May shrugged. 'It's a question that needs an answer. Caspar is not the name of a poor Irish immigrant. I think there's more to this story than just missing parents and, as we know, not all those who are lost wish to be found.'

CHAPTER 16

JINGLE BELL ROCK

Cass had never been to May's bookshop but, as soon as the bell over the door heralded her arrival, she felt right at home. She wasn't sure if it was because of the smell of the books mixed with coffee, the dark wooden bookshelves or the old rugs on the floors. Maybe it was the pot of poinsettia on the oak counter or the dog bed beside the radiator or the mismatched tables and chairs at the back, all scruffy but of excellent quality.

If May's library was her brain in room form, then the bookshop was her womb.

'Hello.' Bastian was seated on a high stool behind the counter, making him eye-level with Cass. 'Coffee?' He hopped down at her nod and went off to the rear of the shop. The place was empty apart from a lady dozing in one of the armchairs and a lone man with a moustache browsing the stacks. The woman looked as if she was a permanent fixture.

'Darcy Cooper,' he whispered, nodding at the sleeping figure. 'Had a late night at Pints & Purls.'

Cass raised her eyebrows.

'It's the local knitting group,' he said. 'Meets at the Station pub on Thursday evenings to knit and set the world to rights. They had a lot to talk about last night with the stabbing.'

'Of course,' Cass said. 'I forget what a little community it is in Blackheath. Everyone in everyone else's business. I'm surprised May wasn't there, drinking in the gossip.'

'May? Knitting? You *have* been away a long time.' Bastian handed her a perfectly made cappuccino and led her back to the front of the shop saying, 'We'll let Darcy sleep it off.'

He pulled a second stool from behind the counter for Cass. She was going to sit across from him, but that felt too much like a job interview, so she moved to the end of the counter instead. She felt absurdly nervous. Cass sipped her coffee, waiting for Bastian to start the conversation. It didn't take long.

'What kind of cancer is it?' he asked.

Cass choked on her foam. 'What? What do you mean?'

'I hope I'm not out of line. I probably am. I couldn't help but notice last night. You've recently had chemo?'

'Why would you think that?' She could feel sweat on her back and was glad that she was sitting down.

'Your hair is thinner than May's, you seem to have some difficulty swallowing sometimes, your nails have ridges, and there are patches of red skin on your palms.' He said all of this quietly and gently, but each word was like a bomb going off in Cass's mind. 'May says that you sleep a lot. You've given up smoking and drinking, which seem to be things you used to enjoy. You're on a nutrient-dense wholefood diet, though might I suggest that you add some fish and seafood. I'm not convinced that going vegan is all it's cracked up to be.'

'Is that all?' Cass asked.

'And you didn't react to the dogs farting last night. You seem to have lost your sense of smell. I envied you that.' He smiled. 'It was savage.'

Cass smiled back. It was a relief that someone else finally

knew. 'Yes,' she said. 'Well done. I finished chemo a few weeks ago. Still getting back to normal, but it seems to have done the trick.'

'I'm surprised you're travelling so soon,' he said with what felt like genuine concern. 'I once cared for someone going through chemo. The treatment is almost as devastating as the disease.'

'I think Minty suspected something was up. She was insistent on me coming home for Christmas.' Cass looked down at her coffee. 'I hate to admit it, but I think Minty was right. Getting here was an exhausting trial, but it is nice to be back.'

'Does May know?'

Cass shook her head. 'I don't know why I'm so reluctant to tell her.'

Bastian set his empty cup aside. 'Are you the oldest?'

Cass laughed. 'By about three minutes.'

Bastian shrugged. 'It matters. You probably feel protective. Is it a familial syndrome?'

'I thought of that as soon as I was diagnosed,' she shook her head, 'but I don't carry any of the markers. It was breast cancer, which is often but not always genetic. I think it was the years of booze and fags that did it for me.' She sighed, then perked up. 'I did get new boobs in the deal though.'

'May, how are you?' Darcy Cooper lumbered up to the desk, rubbing her eyes, and looked at Cass again. 'You're looking well.' She took in Cass's yoga trousers and hoodie. 'That's a new look for you.' Darcy's curly hair was flattened against her head on one side after her nap.

'Darcy, this is May's sister, Cass,' Bastian said.

'I'll be blowed!' Darcy said. 'It's uncanny. I can see the differences now, but...' She looked at Cass with her mouth hanging open.

Cass laughed. 'We get that a lot.' She stood and nodded at her half-full cup of coffee. 'Thanks for that. I should be getting back.' She smiled at Darcy. 'Nice to meet you.'

She was halfway to the door when Bastian's soft voice stopped her.

'Cass,' he said. 'You must tell her.'

Cass nodded without looking back, opened the door and was gone.

CHAPTER 17

HARK! THE HERALD ANGELS SING

The bell over the door rang out their arrival as May and Fletcher entered the bookshop.

'You just missed Cass,' Bastian said from behind the counter.

This was surprising. Fletcher had never heard Cass express an interest in May's shop. Or was it Bastian she'd gone to see? The plot thickened.

'Did you know that Caspar Campbell grew up in care?' May asked, never one to beat around the bush.

Bastian, accustomed to her ways, accepted the change of topic. 'No, I didn't know that. Have you come from Harold's?'

May filled him in on the details while Fletcher eyed the slices of Christmas cake and stollen displayed under a glass dome on the counter. Bastian sourced the cakes from the Bluebird Café in Lewisham which had an excellent young baker.

Bastian finally took mercy on him. 'Why don't we have some tea and cake while we puzzle this out?' he suggested.

A few customers browsed the stacks, but they had a reasonable amount of privacy at the table in the café part of the shop at the back. Under Bastian's management, the online business was booming which meant the shop flourished, even when it was quiet.

The first bite of Christmas cake raised Fletcher's spirits. The cake was moist, the icing and marzipan nice and thick. Absolute perfection.

Bastian held May's phone, looking at the images of the photograph and the baby blanket. '*Jane Eyre*, I think,' he said.

'I beg your pardon?' May replied.

'The writing.' He held up the phone. 'I think it's a line from *Jane Eyre*. Jane expressing her love for Mr Rochester.' He shrugged. 'I could be wrong, but it's easy enough to find out.' He pulled his own phone from his pocket.

'A mysterious photograph with a literary quote, now we're getting somewhere.' Fletcher was delighted by this turn of events. He celebrated with another bite of cake.

'Yes, here it is. It's almost word for word.' Bastian held up his phone to let them see.

All my heart is yours, sir: it belongs to you; and with you it would remain, were fate to exile the rest of me from your presence forever.

'Now, what does that tell us?' May asked. 'A literary scholar? A romance lover? If Jane was speaking to Rochester, does that mean the writer was speaking to her lover, not her child?' She turned to Fletcher. 'What about that ring? I could tell you spotted something when you first looked at it.'

Fletcher took a sip of tea to wash down the last bite of cake before answering. 'The Claddagh,' he said. He cleared his throat. 'It is indeed often called an Irish wedding ring, but its symbolism is more complicated than that. For some, it's just a pretty ring or a love token. For others, it has a number of meanings.' He pointed at the photo. 'Can you zoom in?'

May did as she was asked.

'Now, you see,' Fletcher continued, 'the heart, the crown and the two hands symbolise love, loyalty and friendship, in that order. Interestingly, there's also a Fenian Claddagh without the crown preferred by Irish nationalists who associate the crown with the English monarchy.' May gave him a look that said to get back to the point. He cleared his throat again.

'The important thing to note in the photo is that she's wearing the ring on her right hand with the heart facing inwards. This usually means that someone is in a committed relationship, though not married. If she were married, it would be on her left hand in the same position. If the heart is facing outwards on her right hand, it would mean that she was single. Outwards on her left hand would mean that she was engaged.' He paused before continuing. 'Of course, the rings were quite popular in the eighties. Many people wore them in various ways, oblivious to the meaning.'

May sighed. 'So it may mean that the couple were committed, though not engaged, or it could mean nothing at all.'

'That is correct,' Fletcher replied.

'Brilliant,' May said.

Bastian was looking at the photo of the baby blanket. It was a small patchwork quilt that appeared to be haphazardly put together. 'Some of these fabrics are very unusual,' he said. He zoomed in on the image. 'This looks like a Thai silk, and this is a very intricate brocade.' His forehead was wrinkled in thought. 'I could try some image searches on the fabrics, that might point us in a direction. I can't imagine that these were all widely available. It's a curious combination, not your typical cotton patchwork or the type of blanket made from old clothing by hard-pressed families.'

'Bastian, you're a genius,' May said.

Bastian was quite clever, but genius seemed a bit excessive. Fletcher's information about the ring was arguably just as useful.

'The ring, the quote, the fabrics used in the blanket all point to someone with a romantic nature, what's often called boho these days,' Bastian said.

'Boho?' Fletcher asked. 'What does that mean?'

'Someone who's unconventional, a free spirit,' Bastian replied. 'It's short for bohemian.'

Fletcher considered this. 'Wouldn't that be bo-he?' he said.

'So, we've learnt something about her character, but it gets us no closer to who she is… or was. I guess we don't even know if she's still alive,' May said.

'Boho… bo-he…' Fletcher mumbled to himself.

'Send me the photos,' Bastian replied. 'I'll see what I can do.'

'A free spirit who lived on the south coast in the late eighties, possibly Irish. That really narrows it down,' May said as they walked across the heath towards home.

'It's quite a conundrum,' Fletcher replied. His mind was distracted by thoughts of Sparks and the package that had arrived that afternoon.

'Can you imagine giving up a baby like that?' May said. Her tone had shifted. Fletcher stopped to look at her.

'Are you all right?' he said.

May blinked a few times, then swallowed. 'I can't imagine what that poor woman must've been feeling to desert her child. Where was the father? Are either of them still alive? Do they ever think of Caspar?' Her eyes turned to steel. 'We're going to find them, Fletcher. They have a granddaughter. Surely, they would want to know her.' May strode off towards Greenway with Fletcher hurrying to keep up.

'You know, it really should be bo-he,' he said.

CHAPTER 18

PLEASE SANTA

May checked her reflection in the dresser mirror. She'd chosen smoky-blue cashmere and chocolate-brown trousers for her dinner with Asa. Tucking a lock of her sharp white bob behind one ear revealed a pigeon-shaped earring whose colour perfectly matched May's jumper. 'You'll do,' she said to her image.

She would walk to Asa's place on the other side of the village, drop off her small overnight bag as they planned to stay at his house that evening, then stroll into the village together for dinner. Asa had made reservations at The Rambler, the newest and poshest restaurant in Blackheath. May shivered with pleasure, picturing the evening ahead.

She popped her head into the kitchen, where Cass was sipping another of those vile green juices as Fletcher basted a joint of meat.

'Have you seen the conditions in an abattoir?' Cass was saying. 'Absolutely appalling. How you can possibly eat another animal is beyond me.'

Fletcher paused, looking over his glasses at Cass. 'Is this the same Cass Morrigan who got us kicked out of an all-you-can-eat breakfast buffet in Chicago after eating sixteen sausages?'

Cass shuffled her feet, looking down at the floor, hiding her grin. 'That was a very long time ago. I was young and naive then.'

'*And*,' he continued, 'if I remember correctly, you ate at least half your body weight in bacon as well.'

Good on you, Fletch.

'I'm off,' May said. 'Enjoy your evening. I'll be back sometime tomorrow. Where's Minty?'

'Minty's having her pre-dinner drink in the library,' Fletcher replied. 'Enjoy yourself. I know you will.'

'All-you-can-eat, my arse,' Cass grumbled, as May shut the door. 'Talk about false advertising.'

'Goodnight, Minty,' May said, popping her head into the library.

'You're getting a very early night,' Minty replied, stirring a martini with her finger.

'I'm off to Asa's, remember? Back tomorrow.'

'Ooo, have a lovely time,' Minty said with a wink. 'Give him one for me.'

May sighed. 'Yes, well. Goodnight.'

Finally out of the house and walking across the heath, May felt like a child on early release from school. A whole evening and morning of being a woman and a lover. Not a dutiful daughter. Not a long-suffering sister. Not a responsible friend. Just a woman. A relaxed, desirable woman. Heaven.

'Ms Morrigan?'

May turned to see the young dancer playing Tinkerbell walking beside her.

'I'm Louella. From the panto. I'm sorry to bother you, but... well, I saw you at the rehearsal today and...'

'Yes?' May said, stopping to turn towards the young woman. 'Spit it out, dear.' Asa would be waiting.

'Could I ask for some advice?' Her cheeks had gone very pink.

'Of course.' The poor thing looked so anxious. Did she need to quit the panto? Fletcher would have a fit if he had to replace her at this late date.

'You're friends with Clark Wolfe? I think Fletcher said you were all at uni together.' Louella rubbed her hands together and fidgeted in place. 'I'd ask Fletcher, but I think asking another woman might be best.'

'We were at Cambridge together, yes,' May replied. What was Clark/Milton up to now? It was all too easy for May to guess.

Louella stilled and looked May in the eye. 'Mr Wolfe has generously taken an interest in my career and... well, he's suggested we practise my lines in his hotel room but I'm just not...'

'Oh, no. Don't do that,' May said. 'I've known Clark Wolfe far too long and far too well. Do not meet him in his hotel room.' Could this girl truly be so innocent?

'But, he said some stalker had followed him to Blackheath. That it was safest to meet in his room. Maybe he really does...'

'No,' May said. 'He doesn't. He isn't.' Some things hadn't changed. Clark was still pulling the old "meet me in my room to run through our lines" gambit. He'd tried it with May once, and only once. The nasty brute had walked the quad with a limp for weeks afterwards. Clark Wolfe was the scum of the earth as far as May was concerned. 'Clark Wolfe is not the least bit interested in your career. Clark Wolfe is interested in only one thing.'

'He's very persistent.' Louella looked crestfallen.

May softened. 'You don't need a washed-up old Z-list actor to help you, dear. You're very talented. Clark Wolfe can go fuck himself, pardon my French.'

Louella blushed and giggled.

'Do you have an agent?' May asked. Louella shook her head. 'I'll speak to Fletcher. He has an excellent agent. We'll put some names together for you. A good agent would be far more useful to you.'

Louella visibly brightened. 'Thank you so much.'

'Just promise me you'll give Clark Wolfe a wide berth,' May said. 'The man cannot be trusted, especially with a pretty young woman like yourself.'

'I promise.' Louella kissed May on the cheek. 'Thank you so much.'

May was still thinking about their conversation as she opened Asa's front gate. She would speak to Fletcher about it the following day. He needed to have another word with Clark. Or perhaps it was time for May to step in.

Asa opened the door as she climbed his front steps. 'Hello, lovely lady,' he said in the warm, rich West African accent that seemed to brush gently over May's skin, giving her goosebumps.

She dropped her bags in the entry hall, all thoughts of Louella and Clark dismissed, then stepped into Asa's embrace. His mouth was warm and soft against hers, his body firm and expectant. Dinner could wait.

Much later, May and Asa sat in the candlelit splendour of The Rambler, sipping red wine, staring into each other's eyes, and savouring the moment. They were oblivious to the rowdy tables of work colleagues out on their Christmas dos, pulling crackers and shouting silly jokes at each other.

'*What lies at the bottom of the sea and shakes?*'

'You were lucky to get us in after we missed our reservation,' May said, nodding at the tables of revellers.

'*A nervous wreck!*' There were moans all around one table.

'I supply the security devices for Rambler restaurants throughout the UK,' Asa replied. 'They're very accommodating. Especially when I said it was a special occasion.'

'*What did the turkey say to the hunter at Christmas?*'

'What's the special occasion?'

'*Woof, woof!*' Laughter erupted as everyone in the party started barking at each other.

'Every occasion with May Morrigan is special.' Asa leant forwards to kiss her hand.

May cringed inwardly. He was laying it on a bit thick, but perhaps she was just unaccustomed to being with such an attentive man.

'*What do you call a bunch of chess players bragging about their games in a hotel lobby?*'

'We should get away from here for a while. Somewhere hot,' Asa said as he caressed May's hand. 'Let the sun warm our skin.'

'*Chess nuts boasting in an open foyer!*' There was a pause while the revellers thought it over, then a burst of laughter and stomping of feet as the joke finally landed.

Asa often talked of the future, of them going away together. He'd even used the M-word once but May had immediately set him straight. Another marriage was not in her future. Why would she ever do that again? Christ, she was still legally married to James Faraday. She should probably chase her solicitor about that.

'May, where have you gone?' Asa was looking at her, one corner of his mouth raised in a smile.

May knew that she was being extremely cautious with Asa. It would take time for her to trust a man again, but Asa's gentle persistence was winning her over. 'I'm right here,' she replied.

A sudden commotion at the front of the restaurant silenced the room. A lone party horn gave a mournful wail, then even the rowdy tables of partygoers hushed. There were raised voices at the curtained entrance to the restaurant, but not laughing and high-spirited like the others. One voice in particular sounded full of anguish. May turned in her seat to see the startled face of a man at the front desk. A thick moustache covered his upper lip. He was wearing a coat and scarf, cheeks pink from the cold. His hands, in red gloves, were held out in front of him. The man scanned the restaurant as he shouted in, 'Someone help! Is there a doctor here? Hurry, she's dying!'

That's when May realised, he wasn't wearing gloves. The man's hands were covered in blood.

CHAPTER 19

O, HOLY NIGHT

Fletcher sat in the little study next to his bedroom, making notes in his recipe book by the soft light of the desk lamp. The opened package sat on the corner of his desk. He kept shooting eager little looks at it as he wrote.

Fletcher loved the holidays, but his study was strictly a Christmas-free zone. May had draped every surface of her library in evergreens from the garden. They looked and smelt wonderful, but their clutter was intolerable. Fletcher's space was all calm order. Each book, each paper, each ornament had its place. Every single item in his study was special and significant. His eyes wandered over the soothing neatness as he pondered.

The gammon in Coca-Cola had been a great success, but perhaps a spoon of treacle added to the glaze would give the flavour a bit more oomph? He would make it again for their Christmas Eve meal. Maybe a pinch of cinnamon for the festive season? Nigella served it with a sweetcorn pudding, but Fletcher thought something lighter would be more fitting. They would be indulging heavily the following day, after all.

The phone, charging on his desk, began to ring, startling Fletcher. He looked at his watch. Far too late in Chennai for

Sparks to be calling. He picked it up, revealing an old photo on the screen of May wearing a plastic Stephen Willats dress with Courrèges ankle boots on a typical night out at *The Marquee* over forty years before. In the photo, Rod Stewart's skinny leg, clad in striped trousers, pressed against hers on the cramped sofa.

May's voice was strained when he answered the phone. 'There's been another stabbing,' she said. 'I'm at The Rambler. It was a woman this time.'

Fletcher sat up in the chair. 'Are you all right? I'll come right over.'

'No, no,' May replied. 'There's nothing you can do. I'm with Asa. I'm fine. I just wanted you to know. Tell Cass and Minty. It isn't very pleasant to admit it, but the heath isn't safe at the moment. I don't know if any of you were planning to go out, but… just be mindful. Please.'

'Of course, of course. Are you sure you're all right? You sound shaken,' Fletcher said, as the sound of an ambulance grew closer. The troops were arriving across the heath.

'I'm fine. Really. We're going back to Asa's now. Hot toddies and an early night, I think.'

Fletcher smiled at the image of May cosied up, safe and warm, in Asa's arms. She deserved love and happiness after the last few years with James. The man had been an utter twat.

'Try to enjoy the rest of your evening,' he said as they ended the call.

Another stabbing on the heath. What was the world coming to? He tutted.

Cass had already gone to bed. She'd be up before the rest of them, meditating and whatnot. He'd send her a text with the news. The previous stabbing had been in the early hours of the morning when Cass was usually out on the heath doing her yoga. Putting his glasses on, he peered at the phone screen, carefully typing out the text with one finger. He tapped *send* with a flourish. That done, his thoughts turned to Minty.

He could hear Minty's music playing downstairs. The Mills Brothers? Yes, it sounded like 'Paper Doll'. Minty would be lost in old memories and dirty martinis, a dachshund snuggled in on each side of her lap. Absolutely no chance of Minty getting up to check the mobile phone May made her leave in the niche just outside the library. Ah well, nothing for it. He'd need to go down and tell her about the stabbing in person. Fletcher paused and reluctantly thought about standing up. The leather desk chair had moulded comfortably to his body over the years. It held him most reassuringly.

Finally, resolving to inform Minty of the news, he planted his feet and prepared to stand when the phone on his desk rang. It was May again.

'I think you should come after all,' she said. 'It's worse than I thought. It was Louella this time.'

Out on the heath, it was positively Baltic. Fletcher adjusted his scarf and pulled his wool hat down over his ears as he headed towards the crowd gathering beside the church. The outdoor lights of St Julian's lit the area up like a film set in the centre of the dark common. He spotted May immediately in her long, red Max Mara coat, saved for special occasions. Dinner with Asa Oluso apparently qualified. Asa was standing beside her as she spoke to the detective who'd investigated the first stabbing. May and the detective both looked irritated.

'But I know her,' May was saying. 'She's so young, and she'll be terrified. It's absurd I'm not allowed.'

'I'm sorry, Mrs Morrigan. Only family in the ambulance.' The detective sounded even more exhausted than he had the day before, either from investigating two stabbings or from dealing with May Morrigan. Fletcher wasn't sure which would be more exhausting.

May huffed. 'It's *Ms*, actually.' Asa put his arm around her waist and tried to pull her close, but May stood her ground.

The detective looked from May to Asa, then back again. 'I'll get on with my job if I may, *Ms* Morrigan.' He shuffled off towards the paramedics swarming like ants around a figure on the frozen ground.

'Fletcher!' May spotted him and came forwards, grabbing his arm. 'Poor Louella. She's in a bad way but still breathing. They're taking her to the hospital. Do you have her family's details?'

Fletcher nodded, feeling his pockets for his phone. He kept "in case of emergency" contacts for every member of the panto. 'I believe she lives with her mother.' He extracted the phone and moved away to make the difficult phone call.

As the phone at the other end began to ring, Fletcher watched the stretcher being slid into the ambulance, paramedics scrambling in on either side then closing the doors behind them with a bang.

CHAPTER 20

BABY, IT'S COLD OUTSIDE

'Why don't you go home and put the kettle on?' May said to a shivering Asa. 'I won't be much longer. I want to speak to that detective again.'

'I'm not leaving you to walk home alone when there's a killer around. What kind of man do you think I am?'

May barely managed to stop herself from rolling her eyes. Between her Krav Maga training and the two knives she kept hidden about her person, anyone who tried to attack May Morrigan was in for a nasty surprise. 'I'll be fine,' she said. 'The village is busy and, if you're still concerned, Fletcher can walk me to yours.' She wanted to speak to Fletcher anyway, so this was hardly a concession to her safety.

They both looked over at Fletcher a few feet away, phone pressed to his ear, a pained expression on his face. He must've got through to Louella's mother.

Asa rubbed his freezing hands together, then looked at his watch. 'Fine,' he said with a sigh, giving May a quick peck on the cheek. 'Text me when you're on your way.' Then he hurried off towards the warmth of his house on the other side of the village.

May relaxed at his retreat. It was nice having a lover, but my

God, he cramped her style. She turned and set her sights on the detective, who was busy directing uniformed officers around the crime scene. The detective glanced up, saw May looking at him, and visibly blanched. His eyes scanned the scene, searching for a possible exit route as May made her way over.

She politely stopped outside the crime-scene tape, which had been strung up on poles around the site. 'Excuse me, Detective,' she said. 'I wonder if I might have a word.' He turned away, ignoring her. 'Excuse me!' she said, louder this time. 'Detective!'

He bowed his head. His shoulders rose and fell before he turned around. 'Yes, *Ms* Morrigan. What can I do for you?'

'To begin with, you can tell me your name,' she replied. 'Unless you're happy being called Detective all the time.'

He walked towards May, extending his hand over the barrier tape. A chunky Claddagh ring glinted on his right hand.

'Of course. It's DCI August Armstrong,' he said. 'I should've introduced myself yesterday. Apologies. Please, call me Gus.'

His hand was surprisingly warm, though he wore no gloves, his grip firm. May felt a slight tingle at his touch. She looked at the ring. Definitely a Claddagh, but different to the one in the photo. His was gold, much larger, while the one in the photo was fine and silver. Still, an odd coincidence.

She looked up to find him staring at her. 'Was there something you wanted to say?' His eyes were very dark in the dim light at the edge of the crime scene.

May mentally shook herself, releasing her grip and placing her hand in her pocket to hold on to his warmth. 'It's about Louella,' she said. 'I saw her earlier this evening. She said something that may or may not be important.'

Later that evening, May lay awake in Asa's bed thinking about Louella. As he'd walked with her to Asa's house, Fletcher had said it was just Louella and her mum at home, but the mother was rarely seen and always vague even when she was around. It had taken ages for the woman to understand that Louella had been attacked on the heath when Fletcher rang. He suspected alcohol or some kind of heavy medication. In the end, he'd arranged for a taxi to collect her and take her to the hospital to be with Louella before he headed there himself. Louella needed all the support she could get, poor thing.

Asa had fallen asleep with his arm around May. It lay awkwardly across her waist. His heavy body pressed against May's back in the overheated room, causing sweat to dampen the space surrounding them under the heavy duvet. She felt like a steamed dumpling. *And* he was snoring right in her ear. With gentle effort, she lifted his arm and pushed against him. Asa grunted, tightened his grip and snuffled into the back of her neck. His grizzly beard tickled, not in a wholly unpleasant way.

Asa had been just what May had needed a few months before. The relationship proved to herself that she was still a desirable woman. And, after so many years without sex, it had been reassuring to learn that all of May's parts were still in glorious working order. They'd had a lot of fun.

But recently, Asa had started to become more serious about the relationship. He'd told May that he loved her on more than one occasion (to which she'd replied "thank you" each time). He spoke more and more about their future together but still disappeared without explanation whenever it suited him.

Asa Oluso was a lovely man, but May Morrigan wasn't interested in being tied to anyone. She had enough on her plate with Greenway, the bookshop, Minty to handle and the perpetual divorce to conclude. No, a serious relationship was the last thing May needed or wanted. She was enjoying her autonomy too much.

Asa had started to snore again, taking in deep breaths then releasing them in long, snuffling wheezes. May reached over her shoulder and pinched his nose shut until he snorted, pulled away and rolled over. Thank God. She threw back the duvet, flapping it up and down, letting the air dry her bare skin. She longed to open the window, but the rush of cold air would probably wake Asa. May didn't want to deal with him right then. She needed time to think.

It crossed her mind that if she were home alone in her own bed, she could do her thinking in greater comfort. Another point for remaining single. May sighed and continued to flap. She would have to make the best of it for now.

Two stabbings in two days, both on the heath. One in the morning, one in the evening. One, a married man in his forties; the other, a single woman who was barely twenty. Could it be different attackers? DCI Armstrong would know if the wounds were similar, made with the same weapon. She would need to speak to him again.

Was there anything else linking the crimes? Both of the attacks were at risky locations and times of day. That could point to crimes of passion. A planned murder would surely be less chancy. Passion could take many forms. It could be love, lust, anger, jealousy. But how did passion link Caspar Campbell and Louella Alard? Had they been having an affair and Jocasta had taken her revenge?

May pictured Jocasta in her tidy jumper and floral wellies, flying kites on the heath with their daughter, Tansy. She seemed an unlikely candidate for murderer. Though, if May knew anything, she knew it was impossible to judge a book by its cover or a murderer by her Boden separates. Still, stabbing wouldn't be Jocasta's style. Far too violent. Anyone might be a murderer under the right circumstances, but Jocasta would be more likely to poison someone, or perhaps just one good, clean shove on a Tube station platform. Stabbing would be far too messy and personal.

DCI Armstrong had listened with interest as May told him about her conversation with Louella concerning Clark Wolfe.

Clark was staying in the boutique hotel attached to the Demeter Gardens care home, not a hundred yards from where Louella was attacked. May could easily imagine the man lashing out in anger if he felt rejected by Louella, but would he have attacked Caspar? Why ever would he do such a thing? It felt very unlikely.

Might Clark have stabbed Louella, knowing her attack would be linked to the earlier killing and possibly giving himself an alibi? She didn't think Clark Wolfe's thought processes were that sophisticated. Lashing out in blind anger? Yes. Carefully planning a cunning and successful crime? No, certainly not.

And what about the mystery of Caspar's parentage? *Jane Eyre*, the Claddagh ring, the rich fabrics in the baby blanket. Something started to itch in May's mind.

Asa's phone on the bedside cabinet lit up, bringing May's thoughts back to the stuffy bedroom. Whatever had started coming together in her head immediately dispersed like a wisp of smoke.

Bugger.

Out of curiosity, she leant forwards to look at Asa's phone. He'd received a WhatsApp message.

> know its late but was thinking about you can't
> wait to see you again xx

She grimaced at the lack of punctuation and incorrect use of "its". The sender had used an apostrophe for "can't", why not for the "its"? Texting made people so lazy and sloppy. No excuse for such behaviour.

Beside the message was a tiny thumbnail image. May squinted. It was difficult to see clearly without her glasses, but she was certain the message was from a woman. She read it again, ignoring the errors this time.

May scowled at the screen. Now, what the fuck was that about?

CHAPTER 21

CHRISTMAS PRAYER

It was getting harder for Cass to resist Fletcher's meals. He was such an excellent cook. She could eat chickpeas all day, but they'd never be as satisfying as a nice, thick, bloody steak. Would a little red meat really be such a bad thing?

She'd sat at the table, nibbling her bowl of sweet potato, tempeh and seeds. It was tasty enough but watching Minty and Fletcher tucking into their beef and potatoes was pure torture. The leftovers were in the fridge. It would be easy enough to wait until everyone was asleep, then sneak down...

No. She'd made a promise to herself. No meat, no smoking, no drinking.

Her phone pinged on the bedside cabinet. A text from Fletcher saying there'd been another stabbing on the heath. Jesus, what was happening to the village?

Cass got up and moved to the window. She could see a crowd gathering over by the church. A few minutes later, she heard the front door open and shut before Fletcher appeared, striding across the heath in his coat. Cass was sure May would be out there in the middle of it all. She considered joining them, nosing in on the chaos, then changed her mind.

'Can't be arsed,' she mumbled. Cass had spent a lifetime being at the centre of things. As a child, she was always the ringleader of their little gang. Making up games to be played on the heath and in the tunnels underneath it. If someone told Cass she couldn't do something, she would dedicate herself to accomplishing that very thing. Her determination to prove others wrong had defined her life.

Then she'd found the lump.

The cancer had been a wake-up call. She'd taken a hard look at the life she'd been living and decided it was time to change. Out with the toxic habits and the toxic people. She wanted to start over, to start fresh. No one from her life knew where she was. She'd retreated to another country, a different time. Cass had travelled back to her past to try to find herself. Interesting that Bastian had seen straight through her. Perhaps she wasn't as clever as she thought.

Cass opened the drawer of the cabinet and extracted the crumpled pack of Marlboro Lights. She held the open packet up to her nose and inhaled deeply.

May still had no idea about the cancer, Cass was sure of that. May was too wrapped up in her own dramas to notice anyone else's. Cass put the pack of fags back in the drawer. She would tell May soon.

About the cancer.

About the baby too.

And the rest.

So many secrets.

CHAPTER 22

WHAT A WONDERFUL WORLD

letcher came awake with a start, then deeply regretted the movement. He'd fallen asleep in the atrocious chair in Louella's private hospital room. The chair was hard where it should've been soft, and vice versa. Who designed such monstrosities?

Louella's mother had arrived the night before and spent fewer than ten minutes in the room before declaring she felt unwell and needed to go home. At Fletcher's request, she'd had the decency to tell the hospital staff that he was Louella's grandfather before she'd scarpered. This white lie had allowed him to remain by Louella's side.

Fletcher's neck ached. He carefully moved his head back and forth, wincing at the pain. A crust had formed on one side of his chin where he'd dribbled in his sleep. Rubbing at his face as he blinked, his eyes tried to adjust to the bright overhead lights. They felt sore and full of sand.

Louella lay in the bed, her small form barely disrupting the flat plains of the blanket, her chest gently rising and falling. She'd come out of surgery having lost a lot of blood but in decent shape, considering. Like Caspar Campbell, Louella had been

94

stabbed in the stomach. Unlike Caspar, she'd received help quickly, which had made all the difference.

The door to the room opened slowly and the bossy detective from the night before entered carrying two steaming mugs. He nodded at Fletcher and whispered, 'I stuck my head in a moment ago. You looked like you were going to be in dire need of a cuppa when you woke up.' He handed one of the mugs to Fletcher. Fletcher's shoulder made a popping sound as he eagerly reached for the cup, not caring what it contained as long as it was hot and liquid.

'Thank you,' he said, taking a grateful sip. His parched mouth rejoiced.

'I'm DCI August Armstrong. I should've introduced myself properly before. Apologies for the oversight. Please, call me Gus.'

'Fletcher Redmond.' The two men spoke in hushed tones, aware of the young woman still sleeping in the room. They shook hands. Gus Armstrong seemed to take note of Fletcher's painted nails but made no visible judgement. Fletcher's feelings towards the detective softened a shade.

'How's she doing?' Armstrong moved to the side of the bed, peering intently at Louella's still profile. A look of deep compassion flickered across his face, quickly replaced by the usual neutral police mask. Fletcher softened further.

'She was lucky someone saw her and ran for help. They say she should be fine, though it'll take time to mend.'

Armstrong nodded, his eyes scanning and assessing. 'No defence wounds. Same as the previous incident.' He spoke even more softly, almost to himself.

Fletcher realised with surprise that his mug was already empty though his mouth still felt as if it was full of paste. He eyed the water jug beside the bed.

'Has she said anything?' Armstrong poured water into a glass and handed it to Fletcher.

Fletcher drank it down in one, then wiped his mouth as he

shook his head. 'Not that I know of, and I've been here all night.' He sat up straighter in the chair. 'What's the time?'

Armstrong checked his watch. 'Nine thirty.'

'Bugger!' Fletcher stood up quickly, both knees sounding off like fireworks in protest. 'I need to get to the theatre. I'm sure the Blackheath grapevine will have spread the news about Louella, but the group will be in an absolute tizzy about the production.' His face fell. 'I'll have to recast Tinkerbell of course. Good Lord, we're days away from the performance. Who's going to take her place? They'll have to learn all the lines, the dances, the songs. And the costumes! What are the chances of finding someone the same size? Desi will be working overtime.'

'Go,' Armstrong said. 'I'll stay here.' He settled into Fletcher's vacant chair. 'She won't be alone when she wakes up.'

Fletcher scurried towards the door. He stopped to take one last look at Louella, still peacefully sleeping. The detective sat beside her bed sipping tea like a surly yet urbane bodyguard. She was in safe hands.

'Oh, and Mr Redmond,' Armstrong called, causing Fletcher to stop at the door to the room. 'Are you the father of Louella's mother or father?'

'I beg your pardon?' Fletcher asked in confusion.

'The nurse mentioned that Louella's grandfather had sat with her last night. I just wondered which branch of the family tree you were part of.' He sipped his tea and waited.

'Oh. Um… well…' Fletcher swallowed, his mouth dry again.

Armstrong nodded. 'Never mind,' he said. 'We'll discuss the family genealogy another time.'

'Righto,' Fletcher replied, retreating as quickly as possible.

At the theatre, the company was gathered together in a straggly knot in the centre of the room. Stained coffee mugs and biscuit wrappers littered the floor around their chairs as they discussed the attack on the heath and what it meant for the show.

'We'll never replace her in time.'

'I do hope she's all right.'

'Who ate the last custard cream?'

They snapped to attention like meerkats when Fletcher cleared his throat. So engaged in their impromptu conference they hadn't heard him enter. Half of the group were instantly on their feet, all of them started pelting him with questions.

'Is Louella going to survive?'

'What's happening to the show?'

'Will we have to cancel?'

'Did you buy more custard creams?'

Fletcher raised both hands in a calming motion. 'Louella is going to be fine. She had surgery last night and is resting peacefully.' The tension in the room decreased a notch.

'Does she have any idea who did this to her?' Clark Wolfe thrust himself to the front of the group.

'I don't know,' Fletcher replied. 'She hadn't yet woken up when I left her this morning.'

'Louella is, of course, our first priority,' Clark said, 'but we mustn't let the village down by cancelling the panto. They look forward to it all year long.' He'd forgotten that this was the first ever Blackheath Village pantomime, or perhaps that fact just didn't quite gel with the monologue he was preparing to launch into, given the opportunity.

Fletcher cut him off before he could get started. 'Yes, the play must go on, children. We just need a replacement for Tinkerbell. Any ideas?' He looked around the room expectantly but was greeted only with blank faces.

The door to the theatre opened with a bang as Minty and Desi stumbled in, giggling like schoolgirls. The cold air wafted in a smell of alcohol behind the two old dears. They'd taken the idea of a playdate to heart even though it wasn't even lunchtime.

'Fletcher,' Desi said. 'Are you talking about Louella?'

'No, Des, we were just discussing the state of the economy.' Fletcher couldn't help himself.

'Ah,' she replied, 'once you're done with that, I'd like to talk to you about the show.' She swayed on her feet then scratched her bum, waiting patiently for her chance to speak. Minty hiccupped beside her, wig askew. They looked even more like naughty schoolgirls standing outside the headmistress's office.

'Yes, do go on. We can debate the state of the NHS at a later date,' Fletcher said with suppressed frustration. Desi was, after all, his elder.

'I have the perfect replacement for Louella. Well, not a replacement exactly. No one can replace Louella, she's such a dear girl. But I know someone who would be truly excellent in the role. Someone with an undeniable *joie de vivre*. A definite *je ne sais quoi*.'

'*Oui, oui*,' Fletcher said with annoyance. 'But who is this theatrical marvel?' The whole company held their breath in expectation. Did Desi have the answer to their worries?

Desi turned towards Minty, holding out her skinny arms like a hostess presenting a refrigerator on *The Price Is Right*. Minty adjusted her wig and lifted her chin. 'May I present to you Mrs Araminta Morrigan, our new Tinkerbell!'

CHAPTER 23

HO HO HO

May was in a foul mood. The text message she'd seen on Asa's phone was playing on her mind. It was true that they hadn't explicitly agreed to be exclusive, but May had assumed he wasn't seeing anyone else. She certainly wasn't. Her soon-to-be ex-husband, James Faraday, had had a long affair. The text message poked at a slowly healing wound. She didn't relish the idea of being in the same position a second time.

May and Asa had shared a quick coffee before she'd rushed out the door, saying she wanted to check in on Fletcher and Louella. Asa had seemed more than happy to get to his studio in the loft earlier than expected. He kissed her goodbye on the doorstep, then shut the door, whistling a happy tune. May briefly considered kicking the door open and demanding who he was seeing behind her back. Her hand twitched towards the sleeve that concealed one of her knives. Instead, she went to see Bastian at the bookshop.

Bastian was holding court in the back room of the shop, surrounded by yummy mummies as he poured tea and imparted wisdom. The shop was decked out in holly and ivy along the tops of the bookshelves and a Christmas tree propped up in the window with fairy lights twinkling amongst its branches.

'Rachel Cusk,' he was saying. '*A Life's Work*. Cannot recommend it enough.' He saw May and nodded, sitting the teapot in the centre of the table. 'Excuse me, ladies.' They all turned to watch him go.

'Don't let me disturb your fan club,' May said. 'I just stopped by to say hello.'

He sat on the high stool behind the big oak counter, shifted a pot of poinsettia out of the way, then tilted his head to look at her intently. 'Something's wrong. Besides the obvious.'

'What have you heard about the stabbings?' May asked, ignoring the unspoken question. She fiddled with her phone. 'Fletch messaged me. It seems Louella was lucky. He stayed at the hospital last night, but she was still sleeping when he left for the theatre this morning. Gus was there when he left.'

'Gus?' he asked.

'The investigating detective,' May replied.

'With whom you're on a first-name basis?' Bastian raised both eyebrows.

'It is the man's name,' May said, feeling her face warm.

'Darcy's here,' Bastian said. 'She filled me in.' Darcy Cooper was one of those people who seemed to know everyone and everything that happened in or near Blackheath Village. The woman had eyes everywhere. 'Her aunt's best friend's daughter works on Louella's ward.'

As if conjured by the uttering of her name, Darcy stepped out from behind a bookshelf and joined them at the front of the shop.

'Louella was ever so lucky,' she said, patting at her halo of curls. 'Well, not lucky to be stabbed, but lucky to survive. Being stabbed is actually terribly *un*lucky, isn't it?'

Darcy arranged her face into sadness. 'As for dear Caspar, he was as unlucky as one can get. I feel terrible for Harold and Jocasta, though they're doing as well as can be expected, I suppose. It's been a terrible shock. Poor Jocasta is in a state, but that's not surprising. They were trying for another baby, you know. Such a loss on so many levels.'

May hadn't known the couple had been planning to expand their family, but Jocasta's grief wasn't difficult to imagine. Jo had lost not only the life she'd been happily living but also a future life that was yet to be. May had a deep understanding of that kind of grief.

The bell over the door rang as DCI Armstrong entered the shop. He looked exhausted, with the skin of his cheeks hanging in pouches on each side of his mouth.

'I thought you were sitting with Louella,' May said, her tone more accusatory than intended.

Armstrong held up both hands in surrender. 'Miss Alard is fine. She's awake now but still groggy. I left an officer outside her room.'

'Does she know who attacked her?' Darcy's nose twitched, sniffing fresh news.

Armstrong shook his head. 'It's all a blur. She needs a little time to rest and remember. PC Patel will contact me if Miss Alard wants to talk.' He turned to Bastian. 'I was told you make the strongest coffee in the village. I could use a shot of caffeine right about now.'

'Coming right up.' Bastian hopped down and went to the rear of the shop where he kept the gleaming La Spaziale machine, his pride and joy. As he twisted the handles, the machine hissed and emitted a cloud of steam. Darcy melted back into the book-shelves.

'How are you coping?' Armstrong quietly asked May. 'Not too shaken up by all this nonsense?'

'I'm fine,' she replied. 'It would be nice if you caught whoever is causing such calamity in the village as soon as possible. Do you have any leads?'

Both corners of Armstrong's mouth turned up slightly.

'Calamity. Good word. Do you always talk like a thesaurus, Ms Morrigan?'

May turned her head to look directly at him. 'Are you being impertinent, Detective Armstrong?'

His smile broadened as he met her gaze. 'Impertinent? You *do* always talk like a thesaurus. And I asked you to call me Gus. Please.'

'One extra-strong coffee,' Bastian said, sitting the tiny espresso cup on the counter between them with a thump.

May blinked, swallowed and felt herself blushing. Gus Armstrong had remarkably lovely eyes.

'Thank you very much.' Armstrong knocked the hot coffee back in one. 'Lined in the finest asbestos,' he said, rubbing his chest in response to their looks of surprise. 'Best way to drink it. May I have another, bartender?' He handed the cup back to Bastian.

'Impressive,' Bastian mumbled as he shuffled back towards the rear of the shop.

'All right, *Gus,*' May said as soon as he was gone. 'Do you have any leads?'

Armstrong sighed. 'Not as such. We're working on the premise that the attacks are muggings gone wrong. Probably committed by a local felon.'

'So they were stabbed with the same knife?' she asked.

He shook his head. 'Too early to know for sure, but it certainly seems to be the same size and type of blade. Serrated edge. Probably a steak knife, which also points to a low-level offender who's recently upped the stakes. Perhaps due to drug use, who knows?' He shrugged. 'We'll know more from the lab results in a day or two.'

'Was Caspar mugged?' May asked.

He shook his head again. 'His phone and wallet were left at home. Maybe the attacker was frustrated by the lack of valuables and struck out in a rage.'

May thought it over. 'What about Louella? Was anything stolen from her?'

He pressed his lips together before answering. 'Her handbag and its contents were all there, but the witness shouted when he saw her fall. He did see the attacker, but they were in the shadow of the church. He could only say that they were taller than Louella, wore dark clothing and a woolly hat.'

'That could describe Clark Wolfe,' May said.

Armstrong sighed. 'It could also describe a million other people. The description is not conclusive. Where's that coffee got to?' He looked round to see Bastian, steaming cup of espresso in one hand, chatting with the yummy mummies.

'Yes,' May said, attempting to draw his attention back to their conversation. 'But there aren't a million people in Blackheath Village, only around seventeen thousand in total at the most recent count, one of whom is Clark Wolfe.'

He turned back to face her. 'And how many of that seventeen thousand are over five feet, two inches tall who wear dark clothing and a woolly hat?'

'Well.' She tapped her chin. 'The average age of residents in Blackheath is forty. If we extrapolate that out then–' She stopped talking when she noticed he was smiling again. 'You're being facetious,' May said.

'On second thoughts, I think you're more like an encyclopaedia than a thesaurus,' Armstrong replied. He suddenly seemed very close. She could feel his warm breath on her face and smell the masculine scent of his aftershave. 'Remember those? I used to love flicking through an encyclopaedia.'

'I have a very nice set of encyclopaedias at home,' May said. 'Leather-bound.'

'I bet you do,' Armstrong replied, so quietly it was almost a whisper.

'Apologies!' Bastian's arm reached between them again, setting the second cup of coffee on the counter. 'Got held up with some other customers.' He looked from May to Armstrong, then quickly withdrew and moved back towards the mums, peeking over his shoulder as he went.

Armstrong picked up the cup, throwing the hot coffee back the same as before. 'Ah,' he said with a sigh. 'Back to work.' He placed a ten-pound note on the counter. 'Thanks very much for the coffee, Mr Lovelace. Good day, *Ms* Morrigan.' He tipped an imaginary hat and was gone.

'What an infuriating man,' May said as she watched him go.

Bastian was already back at her side. 'But quite attractive in a rugged sort of way. Wouldn't you say?' He looked at May from the corner of his eye.

'Do shut up, Bastian,' May replied, resisting the urge to fan herself.

CHAPTER 24

CHRISTMAS COOKIES

'Of course, you'd be wonderful as Tinkerbell,' Fletcher said as he and Minty crossed the heath at a snail's pace. She was ninety-six, after all. 'It's just that, are you sure it's not too much to ask? I don't want to take advantage of your kindness.'

Having Minty in the panto would be a disaster. She'd be sneaking in booze, getting everyone tipsy at rehearsals, forgetting her lines, turning the whole thing into a shambles. *More* of a shambles than it already was. And could she even carry a tune? Fletcher had never heard Minty properly sing. Tinkerbell had a solo towards the end of the show. Fletcher had adapted a version of Billie Eilish's 'Bad Guy' for the panto. It was perfect for the wedding scene and Captain Hook's denouement. Louella did a brilliant job with it. Her sweet demeanour contrasting with the lyrics made it very funny. Could Minty pull it off? There wasn't enough time to change the song if she couldn't. It was yet another thing to add to his ever-growing list of concerns.

Minty leant on his arm as she pottered along. 'It's my pleasure, Fletcher dear,' she said. 'I'm delighted to help out. It'll get me out of the house a bit. Tell me, that nice man playing the piano. Is he married?'

So that was it. Fletcher should've known there'd be a man involved. 'Do you mean Cecil?' he asked. Cecil Boudreaux was a volunteer from Demeter Gardens. A painter and decorator in a previous life, he was overseeing the musical accompaniment for the show. 'I believe he's a widower.' He had some memory of a "her-indoors-God-rest-her-soul" being mentioned once or twice.

Minty nodded thoughtfully and patted his arm. 'Yes, I'd be more than delighted to help you out.'

Fletcher pressed his lips together and closed his eyes. He needed to speak to May.

In the kitchen of Greenway, May was baking. Fletcher almost passed out from the shock of it.

'What are you doing?' he said, watching her remove a tray of biscuits from the oven. 'Are you ill?'

May rolled her eyes, then tried to brush the hair off her forehead. The oven mitt she was wearing got in the way, so she shook it off, then tried again. 'What does it look like I'm doing? I'm making biscuits,' she said. 'Like the ones we bought in Cologne at the Christmas market.'

The kitchen looked like a baking war zone. Flour dusted every surface, eggshells dribbled onto countertops. A mixing bowl, crusty with dough, floated in the sink, and every spoon in the house was in a muddle on the kitchen side flecked with dough and flour. 'So you are,' he said.

On the kitchen table was a plate of pristine lebkuchen biscuits. The room was heavy with the scents of cinnamon, nutmeg and clove. He reached out for one.

'Don't touch those!' May said. 'They're for Asa. You can have one of these.' She held out the tray. 'They're still warm.'

He gingerly took a biscuit, still soft with the heat from the oven. 'They're delicious!' he said after taking a careful bite.

'You don't have to sound so surprised,' May said. 'I *can* bake. I just choose not to. It's such a messy business.' She had a streak of flour across one cheek from the discarded oven mitt.

'Yes,' Fletcher said, taking a second biscuit. 'So I see. What's the occasion?'

'I just felt like doing something nice for Asa.' She had that odd twinkle in her eye. Fletcher clocked it just as she turned away.

'What's going on?' he asked. He looked at the biscuit in his hand. 'What did you put in these biscuits?' He dropped it back onto the tray.

'Don't be silly,' May said, draining then refilling the deep Belfast sink with hot water and dropping spoons into it. 'Just the usual flour, sugar, butter, spices, blah, blah, blah.'

He looked at the biscuits on the kitchen table. 'And what about those?'

May turned to look at him. 'Those are for Asa. Please don't eat *those* biscuits.'

He didn't dare ask any more.

'Shall I make tea?' Fletcher asked instead. May was busy scrubbing spoons but nodded in reply.

'Does it really matter if Minty is Tinkerbell?' The kitchen was clean, the tea was hot, and the biscuits were still warm. May and Fletcher sat at the kitchen table. The streak of flour remained on her face. Asa's lebkuchen had been placed over by the Aga out of reach. Fletcher's gaze returned to them again and again as they talked. 'Just trim the part right back,' May continued. 'I don't think you have much choice. You can't have Peter Pan without Tinkerbell and the show is just over a week away.'

Fletcher groaned. 'Why did I ever agree to do this blasted panto?'

'Vanity,' May replied.

Fletcher humphed. 'You could be right about that.'

'Just roll with it,' May said. 'Minty might surprise you.'

It was true that the Morrigan women were full of surprises. One could almost say that the ability to astonish was handed down along with the Blue Willow china when it came to the Morrigans.

'A ninety-six-year-old Tinkerbell is funny before she even opens her mouth. Just cut her lines down, reassign some songs. You can make it work, Fletch.'

He nodded. 'Perhaps.'

'Of course, I'm right,' May said.

The kitchen door opened and Minty swanned in wearing a green sequinned dress and rhinestone tiara. 'All you need is faith, trust and a little bit of pixie dust.' She chucked a handful of glitter at them.

May and Fletcher coughed and spluttered, swiping at their faces to remove the glitter. It landed in their tea, on the biscuits, covering the table and the floor surrounding it. The whole area sparkled. 'I just cleaned this kitchen!' May said.

Minty turned on her heel, heading for the door. 'Every time a child says, "I don't believe in fairies" there is a fairy somewhere that falls down dead.'

'I DON'T BELIEVE IN FAIRIES,' May and Fletcher shouted.

Minty popped her head back into the kitchen. 'You are not children.' She threw another handful of glitter in their direction and disappeared.

May and Fletcher silently looked at each other across the table as they twinkled under the overhead lights. The tea was spoilt, the biscuits ruined.

'Are you very sure euthanasia isn't an option?' Fletcher said. He spluttered as glitter dribbled out of his nose.

CHAPTER 25

WE THREE KINGS

*A*fter cleaning the kitchen again with Fletcher's help, May showered, watching glitter swirl down the plughole. More glitter floated in the currents of warm air created by the hair dryer. Removing it all was going to be a long process. Oh well, it *was* Christmas. If there was any time when it was acceptable to literally sparkle, the holidays were it.

May inspected herself in the mirror, turning her head this way and that. She looked well. Her hair, though white, was still reasonably thick. Her skin was still smooth, apart from a perfectly reasonable number of wrinkles. May's favourite beauty secret was to always carry a few extra pounds. The added weight plumped up the skin so nicely.

Did it matter if Asa was seeing other people? May wasn't ready for a big relationship. She enjoyed the time she spent with him though she didn't want to be joined at the hip in any way. It was his choice of secrecy that bothered her, the feeling that he was going behind her back. That *was* a problem. She would speak to him about it soon. In the meantime, she'd deliver her special biscuits.

Back in the kitchen, May fed Bess and George, adding a

dollop of yoghurt to their bowls to help with George's canine IBS. The poor old girl was growing elderly and falling apart like the rest of them. May stroked George's long back, smooth as a seal's. Even in her lowest times, the dogs had provided May with much-needed moments of contentment. They were such indispensable blessings.

Asa's biscuits were on the kitchen side, well out of Minty's firing range, and remained unglittered. May counted them into a wax paper bag decorated with Christmassy red-and-white stripes. She stopped and counted them again. Two were missing.

Fletcher wouldn't have touched them for all the tea in China. Cass had given up sugar, gluten, dairy and joy. Minty must be the culprit. May shook her head. Serves Minty right. She would get her comeuppance soon enough.

As May was putting on her coat in the entry hall, Minty floated through, still in fairy mode.

May jumped out of her reach. 'If you throw glitter on me again, I will burn this house down with you in it,' she said.

Cass stepped out of the downstairs loo drying her hands on a towel, glitter sparkled around her damp hairline. 'I'll provide the matches,' she said.

'Don't get your knickers in a twist,' Minty replied. 'I'm all out of glitter, so you can both relax.'

'Are you going out?' Cass asked. 'I was hoping to have a word.'

'I won't be long,' May said. She looked Minty over. 'How are you feeling?'

Minty stopped at the door to her room. 'I'm fine. Just going for a little lie-down. Being a fairy is hard work.'

'Tell me about it,' Fletcher said with a sigh, coming out of the library. 'Where are you off to?' he asked, looking at May.

'I'm just popping into the village,' May said. 'I'm sure you can all survive without me for an hour or so.' She collected the post from the mat, shoved it into her Kelly handbag next to the biscuits and set off, leaving Cass and Fletcher to commiserate over Minty's twinkly attacks.

The winter sun had already set as May crossed the heath, ushering in colder winds along with the darkness. Thoughts of the killer at large flitted into May's thoughts, but it was still early and the heath was busy. She tugged her scarf a little tighter then patted her sleeve to check that her blade was in its usual place. She was perfectly safe.

Blackheath Village glowed with fairy lights, draped across the streets from rooftop to rooftop and threaded through the branches of trees on the edge of the green. The local businesses clubbed together to fund the lights along with the Christmas Eve procession every year. It was a time, not just for family, but for community as well.

At Asa's, she dropped off the biscuits. He answered the door in paint-spattered dungarees. May was tempted to stay and see what he had on underneath the overalls but stuck to her plan, giving him a peck on the cheek.

'I had no idea you were such a domestic goddess,' Asa said, peeking into the bag.

'I'm not,' she replied. 'Don't get any ideas. I just had a festive urge to bake.'

'Are you sure you won't come in for a cup of tea?' He'd already removed a biscuit and taken a bite.

May smiled. 'Not this time. I'll text you.'

He nodded, mouth full of biscuit, as he closed the door.

She made her way back to the bookshop. Late afternoons were usually quiet in winter with everyone rushing home in the dark after school pick-up. May wanted a quiet place to sit for a bit and think. Greenway, usually her haven, was too full to provide that kind of peace.

Bastian raised a hand in welcome as she entered but

continued to help the customer at the desk. It sounded as if they were discussing World War II, a topic that didn't interest May. When it came to history, her interests were more in the ancient past, not things that had happened in her own lifetime.

She made herself a cup of coffee and settled in her favourite seat, a wingback chair at the window overlooking the heath. Remembering the post in her bag, she extracted the stack of mail and started sorting through it while she allowed the coffee to cool a bit.

There were brochures from an estate agent offering his help if she ever chose to sell her house and a guttering company that would be in her area and would love to clean her gutters.

'I'm sure you would,' she said under her breath.

Flyers for takeaways, a mobile car valet, and a local meeting of the Jehovah's Witnesses.

Then, a more official-looking envelope. May stopped. This must be it.

She'd had a number of emails that she'd refused to open. They'd decided to let her know the old-fashioned way: Royal Mail.

May opened the envelope and slid out a single piece of paper. The date of her divorce hearing was scheduled for Monday, two days away.

'You're looking pensive.' Bastian sat in the matching chair across from her. 'Anything I can help with?'

May shook her head. 'It's this bloody divorce. The hearing is on Monday.'

Bastian nodded. 'I suppose it will be the end of it, one way or another. And every ending is also a new beginning.'

May looked at him and made a face. 'Have you been reading memes on Instagram again?'

He laughed. 'Fair enough. Trite, but true. It's the final hurdle, then you never have to see him again.'

What a delicious thought to never see, hear or think about James Faraday ever again.

The bell over the shop door dinged and DCI Armstrong came in looking rather serious. 'Do either of you know where I can find Clark Wolfe?' he asked.

May and Bastian shook their heads. 'Isn't he staying at the hotel attached to Demeter Gardens? Fletcher said something about it.'

'We've checked there,' he replied. 'And at the theatre. And everywhere else in the village. No one's seen him since the rehearsals earlier today.'

'I'm sure he'll turn up eventually,' May said. 'They've got rehearsals again tomorrow. He won't miss that.'

He pursed his lips together, unsatisfied.

'Has something happened?' she asked. 'Do you think he's in danger?'

Armstrong sighed. 'Quite the opposite. Miss Alard started talking. She says Clark Wolfe is the person who stabbed her.'

CHAPTER 26

DJ PLAY A CHRISTMAS SONG

Fletcher stood in front of the open kitchen pantry, hands on hips, damp towel still wrapped around his head in a wonky turban. He really wasn't in the mood to cook, but they had to eat. Could he get away with cheese toasties and tomato soup? There were a few leftover jars of Sparks's summer tomatoes. Whizzed up with a bit of basil and some double cream, they'd make a lovely soup.

Wait, Cass didn't eat cream. Or cheese, for that matter. Bugger. What did one put in a vegan toastie? Butter and sawdust? No. No butter either. Fletcher sighed. What a way to live.

May rushed into the kitchen. 'I've just seen Gus at the shop. He says Clark stabbed Louella. Do you know where he is?'

'Slow down,' Fletcher replied, staggering back. 'Who's Gus?'

'Out of everything I just said, that's what stuck? Gus?' May shook her head. 'Gus Armstrong is the detective.' She spoke slowly, as if to a child. 'Louella started talking at the hospital. She says Clark stabbed her.'

'Yes, yes,' Fletcher said. 'I heard that bit too. Have they arrested Clark? Christ on a bike, I'll have to cancel the panto. No

114

Tinkerbell, no Dame.' He pulled out a chair and plopped down. 'Perhaps it's for the best.'

'Fuck the panto,' May said. 'This is about Louella. They can't find Clark. Do you know where he could be? Did he say he was going anywhere after the rehearsal?'

Fletcher tried to think back. Christ, had the rehearsal taken place just a few hours ago? It was all jumbled up with the day before in his brain. The night spent on the uncomfortable hospital chair hadn't felt like a night at all. Fletcher was living one long, exhausting day. Clark had been at the rehearsal, he'd been a bloody nightmare, disagreeing with Fletcher's direction and criticising the other performers. Fletcher couldn't recall him saying anything about what he was planning for the evening. He said this to May. She sat down in the chair across from him.

'Does he have any friends in the area?' She thought for a moment. 'Does he have any friends at all? He could've taken a train into town, down to the coast, anywhere really.'

Minty pranced into the kitchen, no longer in the green sequins, wearing one of her best dresses in red velvet. She took a bottle of gin out of the cupboard and placed it in her handbag. The bottle was far too big for the bag and poked out of the top of it. Minty hoisted it over her arm and turned to go.

'Where do you think you're off to?' May asked.

Minty stopped, sighed heavily. 'If you must know, I have a date.'

'You're not walking across the heath in the dark,' May said, standing up. 'Someone is stabbing people and you would be a ridiculously easy target.'

'I'd like to see them try.' Minty turned and extracted the big butcher knife from her bulging handbag. 'I'd make mincemeat of them.'

'Oh, for God's sake!' May reached over and easily took the knife from Minty's hand. 'You can't go out carrying a big knife in your bag. Have you completely lost your mind?'

'It's for self-defence,' Minty said with indignation. 'It's not like I'm going to be stabbing people for fun.'

Fletcher rested his head on the table. Life at Greenway was increasingly like living in a madhouse.

'And anyway,' Minty continued. 'I'm not walking across the heath. Cecil is a gentleman. He's sending a car for me.'

'And where will you be?' May asked.

Minty pouted. 'There's a Christmas dinner dance at Demeter Gardens. I'll be there all evening.'

'Is your phone charged?'

'Yes, of course.'

'Show me,' May said.

Minty rolled her eyes but took her mobile out of the bag and showed it to May.

'Fine,' May said. 'What time will you be home?'

'None of your bloody business!'

'That's fine,' May replied. 'I'll put the chain on when I go to bed. Take a blanket with you. It's cold on the heath.'

They stared at each other for a moment.

'By midnight,' Minty said, breaking the silence.

'And you'll get a car back?'

'Yes.'

May nodded and sat down. 'Have a lovely evening.'

Fletcher looked up when he heard the kitchen door shut with a bang. He spotted a fleck of glitter out of the corner of his eye. Brushing it off his cheek, he sat up when May stood again.

'I can't sit still,' she said. 'I need some fresh air. Coming?'

Bess and George jumped up from their bed beside the Aga and followed them into the hallway.

'Where are we going?' Fletcher asked as they put on their coats and located the dog leads. 'Not out on the heath?'

'The Cretin asked me to water his plants while he's away.' She rummaged through the drawer of the hall table and pulled out a set of keys, then checked her pockets for her phone. 'Bring the torches,' she said.

They walked out of the gate at Greenway, turned right and ten seconds later entered Geoffrey Crighton's front garden. The Cretin lived in a Blackheath landmark, a huge modernist 1960s glass-and-metal building with floor-to-ceiling windows, vaulted ceilings and open-plan rooms. It was a beautifully designed building that deserved to be celebrated and understood. Unfortunately, The Cretin was capable of neither.

'His place looks as if it's been furnished by a well-trained monkey with too much money,' May said as she unlocked the front door. The hall lights were on and the alarm pad in the entrance started to beep. May tapped in a few numbers and the house fell into darkness with a gentle electronic moan. She switched on one of the torches.

'What did you do?' Fletcher asked, following close behind her, the dogs still on their leads.

'I must've become confused and turned off the whole system by mistake. Old ladies are prone to such things, you know.' She winked, her face ghostly in the torchlight. 'The Cretin has cameras all over the house.' She rolled her eyes. 'Let's get started.'

May walked off into the house leaving Fletcher in darkness. He trotted to keep up, switching on his torch. The dogs pulled at their leads, sniffing the air for the familiar scent of Winston, Geoffrey's bulldog. 'Has he taken Winston with him?' Fletcher asked. The light from May's torch dimmed as she disappeared into one of the rooms on the ground floor. Fletcher found her in the study opening the drawers of an enormous desk. She took a passport out of the top drawer and placed it at the back of one of the lower drawers.

'Geoffrey and Winston have both gone to see Mater and Pater for the holidays,' May said.

The room felt as if it was part of a completely different house. The walls were panelled in dark wood, bookshelves lined one wall. The leather-bound spines of the books looked as if they'd been purchased by the yard. A huge globe sat in one corner. May opened the globe, revealing a mini-bar. 'It's like a film set that's been dropped into this place,' Fletcher said. 'The architects must be spinning in their graves.'

May extracted a bottle from the mini-bar, then opened a door revealing a small loo. 'This is for that pompous speech he gave in Parliament chastising the nation for not being green enough, when we know he doesn't even recycle.' She emptied half of the bottle down the sink, refilled it with tap water and replaced it in the bar. 'Geoffrey bought this room, panelling and all, at an estate sale and had it rebuilt here. He told me all about it with great pride. Come on,' she said, bustling out of the room.

Fletcher took one last look at the study, the heavy panelled walls battling with the light, lofty ceiling. It gave him architectural nausea.

'Tell me more about Louella and Clark,' he said, letting the dogs off their leads. They shot off into the darkness in search of Winston's toys and food bowl. 'Is she certain that it was Clark who stabbed her?'

He followed May upstairs to The Cretin's bedroom. The view over the heath from the big windows was magnificent. May was huffing and puffing as she pulled the duvet off the bed. She removed the flat sheet, turned it halfway so that it was a couple of feet short from the foot of the bed, then arranged the duvet on top again.

'Gus says she's sure. She told him that she hadn't been comfortable meeting Clark in his hotel room as he'd suggested, but when he wouldn't let up, she said they could go for a walk on the heath to talk instead. Clark came onto her almost immediately, she gently rejected him, and he snapped.' She moved over to a set of shelves that held a collection of DVDs.

'This is for his utter lack of compassion and voting against free school meals for all children,' May said as she began selecting

DVDs, opening the cases and switching the discs before placing them back on the shelves.

'Why did he have a knife with him?' Fletcher asked.

'Who knows? Maybe he planned it. They need to find him, then they can ask all those difficult questions.' She headed back towards the stairs. 'Did you notice that Gus wears a Claddagh?' she said over her shoulder as she trotted downstairs. 'It's not the same as the one in Caspar's photo, but it's interesting. Of course, it could just be that I have Claddaghs on the brain and am noticing them more than I normally would.'

The dogs had discovered a few crumbs in Winston's bowl in the kitchen and were contentedly licking it clean. May opened the cupboards one by one until she found half a bag of sugar with a teaspoon poking out of the top. The Cretin didn't bother with a sugar bowl. She continued searching with the torch until she found a bottle of Saxa Fine Salt and a bowl.

He watched May empty half the salt into the bowl, then refill the bottle with sugar before pouring the salt into the sugar bag and giving them both a good shake. 'This is for accepting the speaker's fee and appearing at that dreadful Far Right dinner. Did you know that group actually campaigned to have all first-generation immigrants deported?'

Nothing Geoffrey Crighton did surprised Fletcher. 'Do you think Clark stabbed Caspar?' Fletcher asked.

'I can't imagine why he would,' she said. 'As far as I'm aware, they didn't know each other at all.' She placed the salt and sugar back in the cupboard. 'Bodie,' she said. The little pod on the kitchen side lit up. 'Set up a routine alarm for 3am to James Brown's "I Feel Good" at maximum volume.' The pod blinked green in reply. 'The Abode app,' she said to Fletcher, pointing at the pod, 'controls the whole house.'

'Bodie,' May said again. 'Set up a routine alarm for 4am with the following message in a male voice at maximum volume, "Get up you lazy bastard and feed me. Love, Winston."' The pod blinked green in agreement. 'That's for making a fortune from the morning-after pill in the States, then using the money to campaign for limiting terminations here in the UK. What a contemptuous, entitled twat.'

It was only when May was resetting the alarm as they left the Cretin's house that Fletcher realised not a single plant had been watered.

CHAPTER 27

I SAW MOMMY KISSING SANTA CLAUS

*J*ust after midnight, May sat by the fire in her library still waiting for Minty to come home. The dogs stretched in their bed at her feet. Fletcher had retreated upstairs after their visit to The Cretin's house, intending to get an early night. May and Asa had made tentative plans to get together for a drink, but he'd cancelled at the last minute. She thought about his text again.

Rain check on drinks tonight. Not feeling too good.

She smiled to herself. The biscuits were working their magic.

'What are you grinning about?' Cass came into the library and plopped into the chair across from May.

'Just an amusing text from Asa,' May replied. 'Any plans for this evening?' It was a silly question. Cass had barely left the house since her arrival. She seemed to haunt the place, popping up where she was least expected.

Cass shook her head slowly once or twice then gazed into the flames. She seemed to be moving in slow motion. Her eyes were pink, the pupils enormous.

'Have you taken something?' May asked.

Cass's eyes flicked towards May. Her head followed a second

later. 'Just some gummies. Had an upset stomach. They sometimes help.'

'Where on earth did you get cannabis gummies?' May asked.

'Smuggled them over from the States. It's legal in New York.' Cass's arm slipped off the armrest. She placed it back with a sigh and turned towards the fire again.

'Got any more?' May asked.

'Lots.' Cass fished around in the pocket of her oversized cardigan, rustling what sounded like a cellophane wrapper, then handed May two small, round orange pastilles.

May popped them into her mouth, chewed and swallowed. They tasted like peaches made of plastic.

'Oh,' Cass said. 'I wouldn't have taken both of them, but you go, girl.' She raised a fist in support, then flopped it back down in her lap.

'What do you mean? Have I taken too much?'

Cass shrugged slowly. 'I guess we'll find out.' She smiled at May. 'Seems like old times.' It was the first genuine smile May had seen since Cass's arrival. 'Remember when Jimi was in Hither Green? Going to El Partido, watching Elton perform back when he was still plain old Reg Dwight. We smoked a lot of weed that summer.' She looked at the fire, her smile melting away. 'Who knew poor Jimi would be dead so soon.'

'Yes,' May replied, 'but we all went to the Isle of Wight Festival first.' She sat back in her chair, her body felt heavy and soft. 'It was like a sea of humanity, all swaying to the music. It's still the closest I've come to a spiritual experience.'

Cass laughed. 'Spiritual experience, my arse. We were off our faces the whole time. Have you ever watched the recording of that performance?' May shook her head. 'You can find it online, catch glimpses of us in the wings, bobbing our heads to the beat. We look like those creepy twins from *The Shining*.' She squinted with the effort of remembering. Her hand went to her mouth in search of a cigarette that wasn't there, then fell back into her lap.

'We were wearing those pink Frank Usher dresses. Why in God's name we decided to be matching, I don't know.'

'Jimi thought it was funny. He bought the dresses,' May said. In retrospect, the idea was ludicrous, but they'd thought they looked so cool at the time. May giggled.

'The guys were all wearing jeans and fringed waistcoats, if they were wearing a shirt at all. Then there's Fletcher in a double-breasted suit and tie.' Cass leant forwards, laughing. 'What was he thinking? He looked like Jimi's banker.'

'Oh, yes,' May said, joining in the laughter. 'He was still in his mod phase then.'

'Confess, May Morrigan, once and for all,' Cass said, suddenly serious. 'Did you or did you not sleep with Jim Morrison that weekend?'

May tried to look shocked. 'I was in love with Bobby. I would never do such a thing.' Then she smiled.

'I knew it!' Cass said, pointing at May. 'The two of you disappeared for ages after their set. So go on then, what was it like? I never had the pleasure.'

It had been over fifty years ago. There was no harm in telling the truth now. May sank deeper into her chair with a sigh. 'Heaven. Absolute heaven. He was the most beautiful man I'd ever seen. That hair, that beard, the absolute poetry of him.'

'There's your spiritual experience,' Cass said.

'No future in it though,' May replied, shaking her head. 'I was in love with Bobby, he was in love with Pam, but what a night.'

Cass sighed. 'And he was dead within a year too. So much young life wasted.' She shifted in her chair. 'There's something I've been meaning to talk to you about.'

'Yes?' May said. Cass looked uncomfortable. What was wrong? Did she need money? The Morrigan Trust provided for both of them. Surely, that wasn't the problem.

'Last summer I was at Bonnaroo to shoot some photos and I was applying sunscreen when–'

'What's Bonnaroo?' May interrupted.

'It's a music festival in the States, but that's not the point,' Cass said.

'Then why mention it?' May asked.

'Can I finish what I was trying to say?' Cass replied.

'Carry on,' May said. She wished Cass would get to the bloody point.

'Fine. So, I was applying sunscreen when–' Cass grabbed her stomach and bent forwards in pain. 'God, I've had an upset stomach all afternoon. Must've been something I ate, but I don't know what.'

May gasped. 'You're the one who ate the biscuits!' She sat up and pointed at Cass. 'Cass Morrigan, I thought you didn't eat such nasty things as sugar and carbs. I have to say, I'm relieved to know you do allow yourself treats.'

'What are you talking about?' Cass asked, her face dripping with guilt and confusion. Then her mouth fell open in shock. 'You made skitters biscuits! How old are you? Eight? Who pissed you off enough to make a batch of those?' She groaned in pain.

May started laughing. 'You'll be shitting yourself senseless all night. That's what you get for taking things that don't belong to you. And don't judge me. You're the one who sent a bullet to Thomas Taylor, engraved with his initials, just because he said you were no Julie Christie.'

Cass laughed, despite the pain. 'Talk about being scared shit-less. He hired Jeremy Howard to be his bodyguard for months and Jere, the idiot, took the job because he was saving up for a new motorbike.' She bent forwards clutching her stomach. 'For God's sake!' Cass jumped up and ran towards the downstairs loo, swearing as May laughed even harder.

A key rattled in the lock and the front door opened.

'What time to do you call this?' May said, walking into the entry hall. Instead of Minty, DCI Gus Armstrong stood there, key in hand. He turned to help Minty through the door.

'What have you done now?' May asked, looking at Minty.

'I'm afraid your mother has had quite a shock this evening,' Armstrong said, giving May a stern look.

Minty didn't seem shocked. She seemed just fine, if a little tired.

'Thank you, dear,' Minty said to Armstrong. 'I'm fine now. I think I'll go straight to bed.' She toddled off towards her bedroom, clutching her handbag.

'I'll come and speak to you tomorrow,' Armstrong said to her retreating back.

'What's happened?' May asked him.

He nodded towards the library doors. 'Perhaps we could speak in there.'

They stood just inside the open doors, the firelight casting warm shadows around the room.

'Your mother is friends with a Mrs Desdemona Meade?' He really was very handsome. In need of a shave, but the stubble somehow added to his rough appeal.

'Desi,' May said, a beat too late. 'Yes, they've known each other for years.' She reached out for Armstrong's hand, lifting it close to her face so she could see his Claddagh ring. 'Is Desi okay?' She felt slow and sluggish. Her lips itched.

'Mrs Meade is fine,' he replied, watching May closely. 'But unfortunately, she and your mother were out on the heath this evening.'

'Were they? Naughty. There's a killer out there. They should know better. Tell me about this ring. Is this your wedding ring?'

'It was.' He seemed flustered by the question, removing his hand from her grasp. 'After my wife died, I started wearing it on the other hand.' He swallowed. 'I believe Mrs Morrigan was pushing Mrs Meade in her wheelchair when they discovered the body of another stabbing victim.' He was trying to sound so officious; how adorable.

'Wheelchair?' May said. 'I've never seen Desi in a wheelchair.

How extraordinary.' Gus was no Jim Morrison, but he really was a very handsome man. What a fine mouth he had, a surprisingly full upper lip.

'Someone called in the attack. I'm assuming it was someone from the care home. We're still trying to trace him.'

'Really?' she replied, distracted by the curve of his cupid's bow. 'Is he all right?'

'Is who all right?' Armstrong asked, looking down at her mouth. 'The man who called it in or the man who was stabbed?'

'Either. Both,' May said, though she didn't really care.

'As I said, I'm not sure who called it in yet,' he said with a grin. 'But the person who was attacked is unfortunately dead. It was Clark Wolfe, I believe you know him.'

Why was it called a cupid's bow? What did Armstrong's taste like?

'How dreadful,' May said as she leant forwards to find out.

CHAPTER 28

HAPPY HOLIDAY

Cass sat on the toilet in the downstairs loo. Bloody May and her bloody skitters biscuits. They used to make them when they were kids then give them to anyone who annoyed them. For the Morrigan sisters, that list was long and varied. Other children, teachers, their own parents. No one was exempt when it came to skitters biscuits. They'd even made a batch for Fletcher when he'd dared to criticise one of their outfits.

May hadn't changed one bit. The question was, who had irritated her this time.

Minty banged on the bathroom door. 'I'm an old woman with a weak bladder who's been drinking gin all evening. There's going to be a puddle on the floor if you don't hurry up.'

Cass rested her forehead on the little sink beside the toilet. 'I'm shitting as fast as I can! For God's sake, there are other bathrooms in this house. Use the WC in the mudroom.'

'It's cold out there,' Minty said, but Cass heard her mercifully shuffling away.

She'd been so close to telling May. A few more minutes and it would've been done. Why was it so hard to say it out loud?

CHAPTER 29

BACK DOOR SANTA

The time difference in Chennai was a pain, but Fletcher and Sparks had managed to devise a plan for a very private video call. Sparks was staying with his extended family in a big house near the Kapaleeshwarar Temple. Four generations under one roof meant no privacy at all. A young cousin was always running into the room, interrupting their calls, or an auntie would be shouting in the background, encouraging him to eat something yet again. Sparks had realised that if he wanted to speak to Fletcher in peace, he would have to wait until the early hours of the morning when the rest of the house would be asleep. It meant a loss of sleep for both Sparks and Fletcher, but it would be totally worth it.

Fletcher adjusted the red velvet hot pants he'd purchased especially for the occasion from his favourite online shop, Eat, Drink and Be Mary. The hot pants had a tendency to ride right up the crack of his arse, but they looked fabulous with the boots, braces and big white beard. He made a very saucy Santa, if he said so himself. Sparks would be delighted.

Fletcher's laptop pinged on top of the dresser, positioned for the best view, as Sparks answered the video chat. His eyes lit up. 'Oh, what a ho, ho, ho,' he said. 'Give us a twirl then.'

Fletcher pranced around in a circle, then turned to smile at the screen, hands on hips. 'Show me your baubles, you naughty boy,' he growled.

Sparks's expression shifted from glee to horror when May barged into the room. 'Wake up, Fletch,' she shouted. 'You're not going to believe what's just happened.' She looked at Fletcher, blinked, looked at the laptop, then quickly backed out of the room without saying another word, shutting the door behind her.

'Oh, bugger,' Fletcher said. 'Something serious must've happened. We'll have to try again another time.' He blew a kiss at the screen as Sparks nodded in resigned agreement.

Removing the beard and throwing on his dressing gown, Fletcher headed downstairs to look for May. He found her leaning against the counter in the kitchen, moodily eating Nutella from the jar with a spoon. Fletcher opened the cutlery drawer to grab a spoon for himself. 'Does the situation require alcohol?'

'What do you think?' May used her spoon to point at the open bottle of Baileys behind her on the kitchen side. Fletcher nodded, gathered glasses and ice, then they took their places at the kitchen table.

'Go on,' he said, pouring Baileys into the glasses.

'I forgot how bloody delicious this stuff is,' she said, licking her spoon then scooping more from the jar.

'Double-dipping?' Fletcher said. 'My God, what's got into you?' He eased his spoon in on the opposite side of the jar.

'Oh, unclench, as Cass says. I don't have the dreaded lurgy.' She closed her eyes in pleasure as she took a chocolatey bite.

'What's so important to have you intruding on my privacy?' Fletcher asked. 'It better be good.'

May's face fell. 'You won't believe what happened. It's just dreadful.'

Minty shuffled into the kitchen from the mudroom. 'Your sister is taking her time in my bathroom. I need to cold cream my face and soak my teeth. Are you telling Fletcher about Clark being murdered?'

'What?' Fletcher said. 'When did this happen? I thought he was just missing.'

'Oh, yes.' May shuddered. 'I almost forgot about *that*.' Fletcher looked at May. She seemed odd, off in some way.

'Desi and I found him, dead as a dodo, on the heath. Big knife sticking out of his chest.' Minty switched the kettle on and got the Horlicks out of the pantry.

'Why didn't you ring me?' May asked. 'You were just across the heath. I could've seen you if I'd looked out the window.'

'And be collected by my daughter? How embarrassing.' Minty shook her head. 'Besides, I didn't know you were waiting up like a demented mother hen. Really, dear, I can take care of myself. I'm old enough to be your mother.' Minty had a unique way of stating the bleeding obvious. 'Poor Desi was in quite a state, old thing.'

'Armstrong mentioned something about a wheelchair,' May said. 'Was that for Desi?'

Minty looked away. 'Yes, that's right. She was feeling a bit peaky. All those old people dancing around made the room so stuffy. We went out for some fresh air, and that's when we found Clark.' She picked up her Horlicks and shuffled back out of the room. Fletcher heard her shout down the corridor, 'Hurry it up, Cass. I need my bed.'

Clark Wolfe dead? The panto would have to be cancelled for sure. Did this mean that Clark wasn't the person who stabbed Louella after all?

May was still happily eating Nutella. 'You know, I would actually kill someone for some Chicken McNuggets. Do you think they're still open?'

'What on earth has got into you?' Fletcher said. 'McNuggets? When have you ever eaten a McNugget?'

'I've eaten McNuggets,' May replied with indignation. 'You don't know *everything* about me, Fletcher Redmond.' She gestured at him with a chocolatey spoon.

Fletcher gasped. 'You're high as a kite!'

'Don't be ridiculous,' May said. Her face immediately contorted in thought. 'Oh, wait. You may be right about that. Cass gave me some disgusting gummies.'

How exciting. 'Got any more?' he asked.

May grinned. 'She said she has lots. I'll go ask.' She stood up, grabbing her phone off the table. 'We're definitely going to need McNuggets,' she said. 'With lots of dips. They must deliver them. It's the twenty-first century, for God's sake.'

On her way out, May paused at the kitchen door. 'By the way, Fletch, nice arse.' She winked and blew him a kiss. Fletcher pulled his dressing gown tighter. He could hear her cackling all the way down the hall.

CHAPTER 30

UNDERNEATH THE TREE

The Chicken McNuggets had been the most delicious thing May had ever eaten. That was true at two in the morning. By nine, she was deeply regretting their greasy goodness.

'Why did you make me eat fast food?' she said to Fletcher. 'You know it doesn't agree with me.'

'*Make* you?' he said. 'I barely got my hands on a French fry. You were like some kind of feral animal, storing fat for the winter.' He pointed at her face. 'You've got barbecue sauce on your chin.'

May rubbed at her cheek.

'No, your chin,' Fletcher said.

She really didn't care. The sauce could stay. 'I'm saving it for later.'

'As you wish.' Fletcher sipped his coffee. He seemed fresh as a daisy, but he'd eaten only one of Cass's gummies and very little of the fast-food feast May had ordered in the wee hours. 'I've got to tell everyone the panto is cancelled at rehearsal this morning. We'll have to refund the tickets. Seems a pity, but I'm sure they'll understand. As odious as he was, Clark was the star of the show and the main draw for lots of people.'

'You can't do that,' May said. 'So many people in the village purchased tickets, and the Players need that money. Nothing can be done about Clark, but you can find another Dame.'

'Three days before the performance? Impossible.' He could be so stubborn sometimes.

'I know someone who knows all the lines *and* the dances, who has experience playing a Dame and would be the perfect replacement for Clark,' May said. She watched Fletcher, waiting for the penny to drop.

It took a surprisingly long time to land. Maybe he wasn't as fresh and clear-headed as he looked. 'Don't be ridiculous! *I* can't be the Dame, I'm directing the bloody thing.'

'Most of your directing work is done,' May said. 'And besides, it's just a small local production. No one expects perfection. In fact, it's the imperfections that make it so much fun for the audience. At least consider it.'

Fletcher just needed a little time to think it over. Once he got comfortable with the idea, he'd be raring to go. May left him pondering at the kitchen table.

Fletcher had had a long career as a professor of art history, all academic and tweedy, but he'd also been a very successful romance novelist. At least, his alter ego Barbara Bouvier had been. Barb had produced a book a year for almost fifty years, was published in thirty-five countries and translated into twenty-four different languages. Barb would've wowed as Widow Twankey, but dear Barb had been laid to rest the previous summer when Fletcher embarked on a new writing career under his own name. Still, once a dame, always a dame. May was certain that Fletcher could dazzle an audience again if he just put his mind to it.

She still hadn't told him about her kiss with Armstrong the previous evening, or about the ring he'd been wearing, though it didn't seem to be important after all. Armstrong had been surprised but enthusiastic when she'd leant in and pressed her mouth against his. The two of them had jumped apart when Minty came out of her room to bang on the bathroom door. Armstrong left soon after.

What did that mean? Was he regretting their kiss? Had May made an utter fool of herself?

Minty bustled out of her room. She was wearing an oversized sweatshirt, tight leggings and leg warmers with orthopaedic trainers. Handbag over one arm, the dogs at her feet.

'Where are you off to? The nineteen-eighties?' May asked.

Minty rolled her eyes. 'Fletcher texted everyone about Clark. We have an emergency rehearsal this morning. It's important to be comfortable and have freedom of movement when one is exploring the depths of the human soul.'

'You know it's panto and not *Waiting for Godot*, right?'

'You know you've got sauce on your chin, right?' Minty said as she pranced off to the kitchen.

May headed for her library, still mulling over the events of the previous evening. Had she and Fletcher returned to The Cretin's house? She vaguely remembered shifting his furniture around and stuffing prawns in the curtain rods until James Brown shrieked at 3am, scaring the bejesus out of them both. They'd panicked and ran back to Greenway. She would need to go back to The Cretin's place before he returned to make sure everything was in order and ensure that she'd turned off the cameras before their little escapade.

'Good morning.' Cass returned from her morning yoga on the heath and flopped into an armchair. 'You've got something on your chin.'

'Thanks,' May said. 'I had no idea.'

'What's with the attitude?' Cass asked. 'Sounded like you were having a great night. I heard you and Fletcher laughing like drains when I went to the loo for the thousandth time. Did you tell him you kissed that dishy detective?'

'What!' May squawked. 'How do you know about that?'

Cass grinned. 'Minty told me. Said she saw the two of you playing tonsil tennis when she stepped out of her room. So, what's the story? Does your boyfriend know you're snogging someone else?'

'I don't have a boyfriend,' May replied. 'Asa and I are just dating.'

'Does Asa know that?' Cass asked.

Oh God, she hadn't even considered what Asa would think. That had to be a bad sign.

'The kiss was nothing,' May replied. 'It was those gummies you gave me. I wasn't myself.'

'It wasn't me, it was the gummies, officer,' Cass said in a high-pitched voice laced with sarcastic innocence. 'I don't think that argument would stand up in court.'

Court. May's stomach flipped. Her divorce arbitration hearing was the following day. She'd managed not to think about it for a few hours. May asked herself for the thousandth time, had she done everything she needed to do to prepare? Yes, there was nothing more to do. Her barrister had it all in hand.

'Your face doesn't look like it was nothing,' Cass said.

'It's not that.' May waved her hand, shooing away the topic of the kiss. 'It's the divorce. The hearing is tomorrow.'

Cass sat up straight in her chair. 'Are you worried?'

'Not worried, just... not looking forward to it.' May sat down on the opposite chair. 'I dread seeing James.' She sighed. 'It's complicated. I definitely don't want to be married to him, but I still feel sad about the marriage ending. Is it possible to not want something, yet still grieve not having it?'

Cass's face went pink. 'It's probably more common than you think.'

'The hearing is nothing but theatre,' May continued. 'There's no way he'll get his hands on Greenway. He's come up with some nonsense about the value he added to the house when he lived here. You've seen the kitchen, it's the one Minty had installed when she married Bertie! The man lives in an alternate dimension. The real issue is what happens to Greenway when we're gone.'

'What do you mean?' Cass asked.

'The house has to be inhabited by a Morrigan or it goes to Greenwich Council to do with as they please. The Morrigan bloodline ends with us.' May shrugged. 'No more Greenway.'

Cass's mouth fell open. 'Are you sure?'

'Yes, of course I'm sure. Have you never read the documents? Cass, honestly, you need to engage with your heritage.'

Cass sat forwards. 'There's something I need to tell you,' she said. 'It's important. It happened a long time ago.'

There was a loud knock at the front door.

'Hold that thought,' May said as she went to look through the peephole. She jumped away from the door, rubbing at her chin and smoothing her hair. 'It's Gus!' she hissed. 'He must be back to interview Minty. You'll have to answer it.' Jesus, he couldn't see her like that.

May ran for the stairs, bumping into Minty on the way. Minty fished around in her handbag, then shoved a bundle of fabric towards May. 'Could you hold on to this for me, dear.'

It was a heavy linen napkin with the Demeter Gardens logo in the corner. The napkin was wrapped around something hard. May lifted the fabric to look inside and saw a steak knife covered in what appeared to be blood. 'What the hell is this?' she said.

'It's the knife used to kill that nasty Clark Wolfe. Hold on to it for me. I can't have that lovely policeman finding it in my handbag.' Minty put a finger to her lips and winked. 'There's a good girl,' she said, patting May on the arm before toddling off towards the library.

CHAPTER 31

WHAT CHILD IS THIS?

Fletcher stood outside the bookshop, dithering over whether or not to go in for a coffee. He'd called an emergency meeting at the theatre so the company could decide together whether they needed to cancel the show. As was his wont, Fletcher's thoughts kept see-sawing back and forth. One moment he was certain they should persevere with him taking the role of Widow Twankey. He'd played her before with great success. He knew all the songs and dances. The next moment he was sure that continuing would be in very poor taste considering that their original Twankey was dead and their Tinkerbell injured. Actually, (he paused one worry to focus on another) could someone be targeting the panto? They *were* two actors down.

But no, Caspar didn't fit into that theory, and he and Louella seemed to have been stabbed by the same person. It was probably just stupid bad luck that two of the victims were in the Black-heath Players.

'Fletcher?' Bastian popped his head outside the door of the shop. 'You all right? You're looking a bit anxious.'

'Just life,' Fletcher replied. 'Nothing terribly serious.'

'I've made a little progress on that baby blanket,' Bastian said. 'Got time for a chat?'

Fletcher checked his watch. He had twenty minutes before he was expected at the rehearsal. Minty would take a taxi and meet him there once her interview with the detective was done. He'd left Cass to chaperone in case Minty needed support. May had disappeared before he left the house.

'Yes, a quick one,' Fletcher said. 'What cakes have you got?'

Bastian and Fletcher sat at the table in the rear of the shop, a green tea in front of Bastian, an espresso and slice of ginger loaf in front of Fletcher. Bastian unfolded an A3 image of the baby blanket that he'd printed off and marked up.

'These fabrics are all either surprisingly old or very good reproductions,' he said. 'I'd only be able to tell the difference by touching them. If you want to get even more specific, I have a friend at the V&A who could take a look.'

'Let's hear what you've got so far,' Fletcher replied as he chewed his cake. He checked his watch again. Turning up late after calling the emergency rehearsal wouldn't be a good look. After the shock of Clark's death, they'd need him for guidance.

Bastian pointed to one of the patches. 'This appears to be a Georgian brocade. The pattern was popular in the early 1800s. This looks like muslin and this, as I thought, is a Thai silk. These patches look like black wool, an unusual choice for a baby blanket.'

'But what does it mean?' Fletcher asked. He wasn't in the mood for a long discussion about unconventional fabrics. In fact, the idea of finding Caspar's parents felt irrelevant to the issues at hand. They should be focusing on finding the killer, not rooting around in the distant past.

Bastian rubbed his chin. 'It's an odd blanket, especially for a child. The choice of colours and fabrics point to the late Georgian or early Victorian periods, apart from the scraps of Thai silk. That didn't become popular in England until the nineteenth century. If the fabric was original it would be very fragile, which makes me think they're reproductions, which raises a number of questions. Were the fabrics chosen especially or was the blanket made from what was available? Who would have these kinds of textiles lying around in the late 1980s? Definitely wasn't fashionable at the time.

'And look at the stitching here, it's very slightly uneven, which points to being handmade, but skilfully done.' He looked at Fletcher. 'Would it be possible to see the original?'

'You could ask Harold or Jocasta,' he replied. 'Though I think they have other things on their minds right now.' He shrugged. 'Though Jo might like to have something else to think about.' He considered for a moment. 'We have a wonderful costume designer working on the panto, Desdemona Meade. Desi knows everything there is to know about fabrics and sewing. Perhaps she could take a look.'

'Good idea,' Bastian said.

'What about the photograph of the hands? Any more info on that?' Fletcher checked his watch. He needed to leave as soon as possible.

Bastian shook his head. 'Not much more than you'd already ascertained. Male and female hands, Claddagh ring on the woman's right hand. The ring is a very common design. Could be old, could be new at the time. They appear to be on a wooden bench on a sandy beach, which isn't surprising considering the baby was left in Broadstairs.' He sighed. 'It doesn't give us much to go on. I think the blanket is our best bet.'

'Thanks, Bastian.' Fletcher stood up. 'I'll let May know what you've told me and I'll speak to Desi at rehearsal about taking a look. I'm off to face the Players now.'

'What will you do without Clark?' Bastian asked. 'Can't have a panto without a dame.'

Fletcher pressed his lips together. 'May had an idea. I'll put it to the Players and we'll see. As they say, the show must go on.'

Fletcher actually felt nervous as he entered the theatre. What if they didn't want to continue? Perhaps they'd want to cancel out of respect for Clark's memory? What if they thought his suggestion was in poor taste? Then he'd definitely cancel. Hopefully it wouldn't come to that.

Or would that be the best thing after all?

The Players were quiet, slumped together around the stage, speaking in hushed voices. The proximity of death had silenced the usually boisterous company. Malin Tanzer, Fletcher's Wendy, stood up when he entered.

'Have you called us together to cancel the show?' she asked, looking gutted at the thought.

Fletcher looked around at the dejected faces before replying. 'I know we're all shocked and saddened by what's happened. First, Louella is attacked, now Clark is dead. No one would blame us for cancelling the panto but, if you feel you'd like to, there may be a way to carry on,' he said. 'If we accept that it won't be perfect, I think we can still put on a show that's fun and entertaining.'

Oliver, Fletcher's Peter Pan, stood up. 'What are you thinking?'

'Well.' Fletcher cleared his throat. 'What if *I* take on the role of Widow Twankey? I know all the lines and songs. We'd need to alter the costume.' He turned to Desi, who nodded her agreement. 'But I think we could make it work.' He looked around the room. Eyes were lighting up and smiles were appearing. Perhaps Clark wasn't quite as beloved as Fletcher imagined. 'Thoughts?'

'It's a brilliant idea,' Malin replied. There was a murmur of agreement. 'We can dedicate the performance to Clark. I'm sure he'd want for us to continue.'

'We've got an extraordinary replacement Tinkerbell,' Fletcher said with a grin. 'It would be a pity not to carry on.'

'Let's do it,' Oliver said. The rest of the group got to their feet and started chattering to each other about what needed to be done.

'Yes, yes.' Fletcher raised his hands to quiet them. 'It's not going to be easy, but we can still put on a hell of a show. Shall we get started?'

CHAPTER 32

THAT'S CHRISTMAS TO ME

By the time May showered, dressed and returned downstairs, Minty and DCI Armstrong had left: her to the meeting of the Players and him to his investigations. Cass was nowhere to be seen, probably lying down again. This suited May just fine. It was the Sunday before Christmas. She had a tradition to uphold. She would talk to Minty about the knife later.

For over twenty years May had kept the Sunday before Christmas just for herself. She'd go into town for any last-minute shopping, then treat herself to lunch and a cocktail at Rules. Once ensconced in the plush interior of the oldest restaurant in London, any nagging worries would recede, and the holidays would truly begin. She'd treat herself to oysters, roast beef or perhaps a rabbit cassoulet, and finish up with a crumble or some sticky toffee pudding. It was her special moment of peace during the busy festive season.

As she strode through the crowds in Trafalgar Square, May mentally sorted through her shopping list: a bottle of Minty's favourite Millesime Imperial from Creed, the new summer hat she'd ordered for Fletcher from Lock & Co, an umbrella from

"

James Smith & Sons for Cass, some new brushes from L Cornelissen & Son for Asa, and lots of nibbly bits from Fortnum's.

Three hours later she settled into the comfortable banquette at Rules, her bags safely stowed with the porter. She'd purchased everything on her list plus a few little treats for herself. It had been a difficult year. She deserved it.

The shops had been packed, but everyone was in festive spirits. May loved being in town. It was the one thing she missed about working at the British Library, that sense that the city belonged to her. So much had changed, but thankfully a few places, like Rules, seemed to be eternal.

As she sipped her champagne cocktail, May watched the smartly uniformed waiters moving from table to table as if carefully choreographed. The lighting was warm, the Christmas decorations were jolly but tasteful, and the atmosphere was one of peaceful elegance. Her favourite table was under the Thatcher mural where she could see out of the front windows and watch the bright day give way to the early darkness of winter.

It was an indulgence, there was no doubt about that, but May felt that little (and not so little) acts of self-love were crucial to a happy existence.

Hours later, she waited for her shopping at the front desk feeling replete, rested, slightly tipsy, and without a smidgen of guilt. Voices filtered down from the upstairs cocktail bar. A woman giggled as she and her partner stopped on the stairs for a kiss. May could see them from the waist down, their thighs pressed against each other, his hand reaching around to squeeze the woman's bottom before they continued to descend. The world was in high spirits indeed.

May looked away to give the couple privacy but was startled to hear a voice calling her name.

'May! What a surprise bumping into you here.' It was the head of the Blackheath Players, Margaret Stout. Behind her was a very sheepish-looking Asa Oluso.

May's thoughts immediately went to the knife wrapped in a napkin in the bottom of her handbag. The knife that had already been used in at least one crime. Then she steadied herself, gave Asa a steely smile and turned to the woman. 'Hello, Margaret. How lovely to see you. Out for a festive drink?'

Did she know that Asa had been seeing May too? Probably not, from her friendly demeanour.

Margaret blathered on about the holidays and her children coming home and what a wonderful job Fletcher was doing with the panto. Her face was ruddy and her breath smelt of spirits. She seemed almost giddy, delighted to be out on the town with a handsome man. May couldn't blame her. Asa was very charming.

May studiously avoided looking at him, though she could feel his gaze warming the side of her face. When May's bags arrived, Margaret's monologue ground to a slow halt. May took the opportunity to say goodbye and hurried out the door wishing them both a happy Christmas.

The rush of cold, fresh air was more than welcome after enduring Margaret's sour breath. May was determined not to let the experience spoil her day. She'd take a black cab all the way back to Blackheath, process what had just happened during the journey, and arrive home in a better mood.

May was halfway to the Strand when someone grabbed her arm. It was Asa.

'May, I'm sorry about that.' He was out of breath, had run to catch up with her.

'It's fine,' she said. 'Go back to Margaret and enjoy your afternoon.'

He stepped back, a look of surprise on his face. 'Really? Are we still on for tomorrow then?'

'Oh, God no,' May replied. 'We're done. It was lovely while it lasted. Thank you very much.' She turned to go, but he stopped her.

'Don't be like that,' he said. 'We never said we were exclusive. If that's something you want, we should talk about it.'

'I'll *be* any way I please,' May snapped. Then softened slightly. 'To be honest, I'm not sure what I want right now, but I do know, without a shadow of a doubt, that it's not this. Goodbye, Asa.' She turned to leave, then stopped. 'Margaret is a nice lady, Asa. Be kind.'

She walked on to the Strand, leaving Asa Oluso standing on the pavement.

The cab home seemed to take forever. May's stomach was in turmoil. The oysters and beef seemed to be fighting it out in her gut. The oysters were winning. Traffic was a nightmare. The taxi kept stopping and starting, making May seasick with the movement. She just wanted to be home where she could wash her face and lie down. By the time May reached Greenway, she was in a foul temper.

'Ah, May.' Fletcher and the dogs greeted her in the entry hall. 'I spoke to Bastian about that baby blanket…'

'Not now,' she said, holding up a hand. 'I've got a migraine coming on. I need to drink a glass of water with lemon juice, lie down, and sleep it off. We'll talk later.' She dropped her bags beside the coat hooks. 'And don't look in those bags.'

'Righto,' he replied. 'You go up. I'll get the water and lemon.'

A pint of water with the juice of one lemon had been recommended to May as a way to ward off a migraine by a dear biologist friend many years before. It usually worked a treat.

'May, there you are.' Minty stopped her at the foot of the stairs. 'I need to speak to you about that little thing we discussed yesterday. You know, the…' She made hand motions like she was Norman Bates in the shower scene in *Psycho*.

'Not now,' May said. 'Migraine.' She really hoped she wouldn't vomit. That was always such a horribly undignified experience.

Cass came out of her bedroom just as May reached the landing. 'May, I've been trying to talk to you about something and…'

'No!' May held up both hands in desperation, then said more quietly, 'Migraine. Must sleep.'

At last, she reached the peaceful sanctity of her bedroom. After washing her face in the en suite, she changed into pyjamas. If she was going to sleep this early, then she would do it properly. Fletcher had left the pint glass of water and lemon on a little doily beside the bed, bless him. May drank it down in one, then climbed under the blankets in search of sweet oblivion.

CHAPTER 33

A CHRISTMAS CAROL

Cass tossed and turned in bed. She looked at the clock again. 2am. Another day gone without having a proper talk with May. It seemed impossible to pin her sister down. May, Minty and Fletcher had each been in and out of the house all day. When they were home, they were holed up in their bedrooms or all together in the kitchen or library. The idea of outright asking to speak to May alone felt too awkward and ominous. Cass wanted the conversation to happen naturally, which was proving difficult.

She looked at the clock again. It was pointless trying to sleep. Throwing back the duvet, Cass decided to go downstairs for a snack. Maybe some more of May's secret chocolates would help her get back to sleep. If she stuck to just eating Fletcher's favourites, then May would never suspect Cass of being the chocolate thief.

Tiptoeing down the stairs, Cass avoided the creaking boards out of habit. In the entry hall she noticed that May had left the Christmas tree lights on in the library – a seam of flickering light was visible under the closed doors. Cass hesitated, then decided to do the right thing and switch them off. She could hear their father's voice in her head. *Sodding fire hazard, if you ask me.* God, he'd been a grumpy git.

Cass opened the library door. A figure was crouched beside the fire brandishing an iron poker. Cass gasped.

'Bloody hell!' May shouted. 'What are you doing up? You're lucky I didn't smash you over the head with this thing.' She turned and used the poker to prod the fire back to life, then returned it to its place on the hearth. The dogs had jumped up, ready to attack any intruders, then settled back down on their cushion when they saw it was just Cass. It was way past their bedtime, far too late to be getting excited over nothing.

Cass clutched her chest, breathing hard. 'Jesus, what are *you* doing up? Don't you need to be in court in a few hours?' She plopped into an armchair, waiting for her heart rate to settle. She'd never get back to sleep with all the adrenaline pumping through her veins.

May sat down across from her. 'I went to bed too early. Can't sleep now. Too much going on in my head.'

'That's not surprising,' Cass said. 'It's an important day. You were married a long time. Too long, in my opinion.' Cass had never trusted James. He was an odd man. She always had the feeling that he was just pretending to be human, constantly masking whatever brokenness lurked deep inside. She met him only a handful of times over the years, and that had been plenty.

May sighed. 'It's as if I'm supposed to be celebrating, but I don't feel like celebrating. I feel sad, like someone died. I don't want to be married to him, yet I don't want the marriage to end. It's doing my head in.'

'If you want to get deep about it,' Cass said, 'someone *has* died. James's wife doesn't exist anymore. That part of your identity is gone, but you're perfectly whole without it. You've got to reclaim your individual sense of self. From what I've seen, you've started doing that already. It'll just take time.'

'I read a beautiful book by Maggie Smith. The American poet, not the British actress,' May said. 'It's about the end of her marriage. She says that life is recursive so all the things she did married, she would do again unmarried. Imagine all the things I've done as a wife. Forty years of living. To do them all over again alone…' Her voice trailed off in thought. 'I'll be dead before I'm able to completely unpick that seam.'

'Firstly,' Cass replied, 'you're the most un-alone person I know. Look around you. You're surrounded by people who love you. And I know I wasn't here much, but it seems to me that you were more alone in your marriage than you are now. Maybe it's not about unpicking the seam,' Cass said. 'Maybe you just continue it with a different colour thread? I don't know.' She shrugged. 'God forbid I ever pick up a needle and thread.'

'I do have good friends.' May nodded. 'And I'm very grateful for them.' She sighed. 'I ended things with Asa today. I know it's for the best, but it feels like that ending is currently causing me more pain than the divorce. Is that insane? So many endings. I'm not sure I can take any more.'

'Referred grief,' Cass replied.

'I beg your pardon?' May said.

'When the grief of one thing is too big to handle, so we soldier on and do our best to ignore it. Then, some lesser loss happens and we fall apart. It's easier to focus on the little thing than it is on the enormous thing. Very common.'

May looked at Cass for a long moment. The weak firelight and twinkling lights made May's skin glow. She looked like the young woman that Cass always pictured when she thought of her sister. 'I'm glad you came back,' May said at last.

Cass's heart squeezed in her chest. There had been a time when she and May had been inseparable. They'd known everything about each other, had shared every secret. Perhaps it was time to rebuild that sisterly connection, if it wasn't too late.

May seemed to make a decision. 'And then there's this,' she

said, reaching down beside her chair to extract something from her handbag.

'How *did* you end up with Minty's old Kelly bag?' Cass asked.

'Minty left it here when she went off to France,' May said, removing a bundle from the bag. 'I've carried it for decades. It's mine now.'

'I had my eye on that bag for years before–' She was silenced when May held out a bloody knife wrapped in a cloth. 'Where did that come from?' She leant forwards for a closer look. The dried blood looked black in the firelight.

'Don't touch it. Fingerprints,' May said, her mouth grim. 'Minty gave it to me. She said it's the knife used to stab Clark Wolfe.' May wrapped it up again and shoved it back into the handbag.

'Why did Minty have it? Why do you have it now? Did she stab him?' So many questions were battling in Cass's head.

May shrugged. 'I haven't spoken to her about it yet. I don't know what happened. She just told me to hold on to it and to not let the detective know she's got it. To be honest, I'm not sure I want to know what she's been up to. I'm assuming she picked it up when she and Desi found the body. Why she would do such a thing, I've no idea. But Minty operates in her own little world.'

'What are you going to do with it?' Cass asked. God, her family was a nightmare. Maybe she'd go back to the States after all.

'No idea,' May said. 'I guess I'll get rid of it. How could I possibly explain this to the police? "Sorry, officer, my mother must've picked it up by mistake and I just forgot all about it."'

Cass nodded. It was a tricky situation. She took a deep breath. 'While we're making confessions, there's something I need to tell you.' She looked May in the eye and spoke as quickly as possible. 'I've got cancer. Or rather, I had cancer. Breast cancer. I had all the treatments, the surgeries, and I've been given the all-clear. For now.' Christ, it felt good to say it at last. 'We're identical twins, so you need to know, but I think it was the fags that did it for me. You might never get it. Are your mammograms up to date?'

'Slow down,' May said, seemingly stunned. 'Cancer? That's why…' She motioned to her chest. 'I just thought you'd had a boob job. My God, I'm so sorry.'

'Sorry that I had cancer, or sorry that you assumed I'd had plastic surgery?'

'Both,' May said. Her eyebrows came together. 'Why didn't you tell me? I would've gone to the States to help. Did you deal with all of that on your own?'

Cass shook her head. 'As difficult as it may be to believe, I do have friends.' She smiled. 'I wasn't alone, but it was absolute shit. I don't recommend it.'

'I can't believe you kept that from me. Did Minty know?'

'Not explicitly, but I think she knew something was up. She was a terrible mother when we were young, but she's always kept in touch, always shown an interest.' The fire was dying. Just a few glowing coals left, but they still gave off a comforting warmth. 'I went quiet for a while. That's when she started telling me to come home for Christmas. She kept leaving long voicemails extolling the virtues of Blackheath in winter. I'm not sure she wants to know what actually went wrong, Minty has never been good with the messier parts of life, but she sensed that Greenway was where I needed to be.'

May raised an eyebrow. 'Was she right about that?'

'Surprisingly, yes,' Cass said.

May smiled. 'So, to recap: there's a killer on the heath, I'm finalising my divorce, Minty may or may not have killed some-one, and you're recovering from cancer. Anything else you'd like to add to that list?'

'Actually,' Cass said. 'There is.'

CHAPTER 34

LITTLE SAINT NICK

May sat back in the armchair, bracing herself for whatever Cass was about to say. What could be worse than cancer? 'More bad news?' she asked.

Cass seemed to think it over. 'I'm not sure I would call it bad news. Just… surprising. Or possibly upsetting.'

'Spit it out,' May said. 'Just rip the plaster off quickly. Best way to go about it.'

Cass took a deep breath. 'I had a baby.'

'Oh, no you didn't!' May squawked so loudly the dogs crawled out from under their blanket to see what was going on.

'Oh, yes I did,' Cass said.

'When? How? Where's the child? Who's the father?'

Cass held up her hands. 'I'll tell you everything I know, but it's not much.'

'How can you not know absolutely everything about it?' May said. Had Cass completely lost her mind?

'It was a long time ago,' Cass replied. 'Remember when I didn't return to Cambridge after the Christmas break? I followed Percy on the Zeppelin tour in the States?'

'I remember you met him at the Isle of Wight Festival a few

"

months before then. Did you get pregnant there? Are you telling me you had a baby with Robert Plant?'

'Yes. No, let me finish,' Cass said. 'I did get pregnant at the festival but, when Jimi died a few weeks later, I put my missed periods down to grief. Then it was Christmas and then New Year. By the time I realised what was happening, I didn't have many options.'

'New Year 1970?' May asked. Her blood had turned to ice. 'I was pregnant too.'

Cass's mouth fell open. 'Isle of Wight?'

May shook her head. 'Just after, when I went back to Cambridge. It was Bobby's.' She'd never wanted to think about that time ever again. How strange that Cass had been fighting a similar battle.

'What happened?' Cass whispered.

'Bobby wasn't pleased. I had to get rid of it. I almost died. It was horrible.' Blood-soaked memories filled May's head. Her chest and throat felt tight. She steadied her breathing carefully. In and out. In and out.

'Didn't Bobby die in '71? Hit his head and drowned in the Cam?' Cass said this quietly, her eyes never leaving May's face.

'That's right,' May said, looking away.

The silence stretched between them for a long moment.

'I need some air,' May said, standing up and moving towards the door.

'It's almost three o'clock in the morning! You're going out?'

'I don't care what time it is. My head is spinning. You're welcome to join me.' May felt as if she was suffocating. She needed to get outdoors. Her head was ready to explode with the information she and Cass had shared. They put on coats, gloves and scarves. The dogs looked at them but refused to leave their warm spot by the fire. 'Fair enough,' May said to them as she grabbed her handbag and opened the door.

. . .

The bells of St Julian's were ringing three o'clock as May and Cass set off across the heath.

'Sounds like someone's having a party,' Cass said as 'I Feel Good' blasted from The Cretin's house next door.

'Yes, it does,' May replied, smiling to herself.

The heath was a vast, dark desert at that hour without another soul in sight. The snow had arrived and was falling in curtains of heavy flakes, steadily settling in shallow drifts. May and Cass carefully crunched across the frozen grass, their breath coming out in white puffs.

'What happened?' May said. 'With your baby. Did you have a termination too?' The falling snow did funny things with the acoustics in the wide open space. They seemed wrapped in an eerie cocoon of white, their voices sounded sharp and close.

'I had the baby,' she said. 'But I gave it away. I was young and irresponsible. I was grieving for Jimi. I was in no state to raise a child. I know it was the right thing to do, but it's always haunted me. It's like you said about not wanting something, but grieving it too. I just hope the child had a good life. I'm sure it was better than anything I could've offered at the time.'

They stopped in a spill of moonlight beside the church. 'Cass,' May said. 'I'm so sorry. I can only imagine what that was like for you. And you've carried that knowledge all by yourself all these years? You didn't have to. You could've told me. I would never have judged you.'

'I know that,' Cass said, looking down. 'It's complicated.' She took a deep breath before speaking again. 'The father of the ba–' The words died in a gurgle.

They'd been so focused on their conversation they hadn't heard the stranger who'd crept up behind them and now had one arm around Cass's throat. His other hand prodded a knife under her chin.

'Good evening, ladies,' the man said. 'This won't take long.

Which one of you is May Morrigan?' He grinned. Madness sparked behind his eyes.

'I am!' they both said.

'Don't listen to her,' May said. 'What do you want with me?' He looked vaguely familiar, but she couldn't quite place him.

'She's lying to protect me,' Cass said. 'I'm May.'

'Shut up! Both of you,' he hissed. 'Your mother killed the best man to ever walk this earth. She took away the one person I've ever loved. Now, I'm going to take away someone *she* loves.' He tightened his grip on Cass's throat. 'I know one of you has cancer. I heard you talking about it with that freak in the book-shop. I'll let that one, the one called Cass, die slowly. May is the one I'm planning to kill now. But, if you don't cooperate, I'm happy to take you both out tonight. Your call.'

'You must be mistaken,' May said. 'Our mother's ninety-six. She's not capable of killing anyone.'

'I saw her!' he shouted. 'Her and that other old witch. They dumped his body like he was a sack of rubbish.' His voice broke on the final word. The man was distraught.

May looked at Cass. Could Minty really have done such a thing?

'Please don't hurt us,' Cass said, making eye contact with May. May knew that look. It was the same expression Cass had when Gerald Feinman had grabbed her at the Guy Fawkes fireworks display one year. The next second he was flat on his back, strug-gling to breathe. May's body tensed in preparation for whatever Cass was about to do.

'We'll cooperate,' Cass said, raising her hands in a submissive gesture.

'Bloody right yo–' He never finished the sentence. In one swift gesture Cass had slipped under his arm and dropped to the ground, swiping his thigh as she fell.

May fumbled for the knife tucked inside the special pocket in her sleeve. *Damn coat!*

Cass was already up with a knife in her hand. Where did that come from? The three of them stood in an awkward circle, each of them brandishing a blade.

'Now this is a turn-up for the books,' Cass said, panting slightly. 'Is this what they call a Mexican standoff?'

May was too shocked to reply. 'Cass Morrigan! I didn't think you had it in you.' She looked from Cass back to the man as a dark stain soaked through his khaki trouser leg. He was staring at May.

'You're May,' he said, trying to step towards her, but his leg gave out from under him. He fell to the ground, clutching his blood-soaked thigh. 'You cut me! How could you do this to me? These are my favourite trousers. I need an ambulance,' he said to Cass.

'You're lucky I didn't have my gun on me,' Cass said. 'You'd already be dead.'

'Gun!' May gasped. 'Oh, for God's sake, Cass. I hope you're joking.'

Cass shrugged. 'So this is the guy causing so much trouble on the heath? Do you know him?'

May looked down at him, bending forwards to get a better look. He was in his forties she'd guess, with a dark moustache. He responded with a whine. She shook her head. 'He looks familiar, but maybe Gus was right. Just some random thug. Now, that is disappointing.' She sighed. 'It's so much more satisfying when it's someone you know.' She looked back at Cass, then froze, mesmerised by the shining blade in Cass's hand. It was a slim stiletto, silver, decorated with golden stars, a twin for the one in May's hand. May reached down into her boot and extracted a second matching knife, then looked at Cass again.

The man whimpered and curled into a ball. 'I need an ambulance! It's not just a flesh wound,' he shouted again.

'Yes, yes. Just a moment,' May said to him, then turned back to Cass. 'Where did you get that knife?'

Cass glanced at the weapon in her hand smeared with blood, grimaced, then rolled her eyes. 'Where do you think?'

'You slept with Jean-Luc? *My* Jean-Luc?' May was exasperated beyond belief. Jean-Luc had been her fencing instructor at university. They'd enjoyed a brief but passionate affair before May graduated. The matching stiletto blades had been his parting gift.

'Call the ambulance, please! I'm dying here.' He started rolling around on the frozen grass.

'I'm afraid to say he wasn't *your* Jean-Luc,' Cass said to May. 'He was *everyone's* Jean-Luc. He probably bought these knives by the truck-load.' She bent forwards to wipe her blade clean on the grass, then tucked it away inside her coat.

May huffed. 'God, men are pigs.' She put her own blades back into their hiding places with a sigh, then looked at the man grunting in pain on the ground before them. 'What are we going to do with this one?'

Cass shrugged her shoulders. 'I say we leave him here to bleed out. Shouldn't take much longer. I snagged the femoral artery. Works every time.'

Every time? What the fuck was wrong with this family? Or did all families have conversations like this? Was everyone hiding their murderous tendencies under cloaks of mediocrity?

'Noooo!' he said. 'Listen, this French fella sounds like an arse. I'm sure you're both better off without him. Can you please ring the ambulance. I'm not quite dead yet.'

May bent forwards to look at him again, her hip twinged with the movement. It finally clicked. 'You're the man who found Louella. I recognise you from The Rambler. Did *you* stab her?'

'No,' he shook his head, 'Clark did that, but I'm sure he had his reasons, though she did seem like a nice young lady. I like to follow Clark. We're friends. He's not a bad man really. I'm sure he didn't want for her to die.'

'You must be the stalker.' May stood upright. 'He's right about

Jean-Luc,' she said to Cass. May tutted, shaking her head as she extracted her phone from her handbag. 'I'll dial 999 but it sounds like you're in this up to your neck. I hope Clark was worth all the trouble.' She turned back to Cass. 'You didn't finish telling me what happened with the baby.'

'What baby?' the man said.

'Not you,' May replied. 'My sister's baby.'

'I don't think now is the time,' Cass replied. 'We've got other things to deal with.'

'It'll take two seconds if you just tell me quickly,' May said, exasperated.

'I don't want to tell you quickly,' Cass said. 'It's not the kind of thing you tell in two seconds. I've waited over fifty years, I can wait a little longer.'

'Fine.' May held up her phone, trying to see the screen without her glasses. She took off one glove to dial the number.

'Wait,' Cass said. 'I don't think he's going to need that ambulance after all.' She knelt down beside the man and felt for a pulse. Looking up at May, she shook her head. 'Too late.'

'Shit,' May said. 'Should I ring the police?'

'I've got a better idea,' Cass replied. 'Give me your handbag.'

CHAPTER 35

MERRY CHRISTMAS

Fletcher sipped his coffee at the kitchen table, fretting about May and her day in court, castigating himself for not being there with her, then switching to worrying about the rehearsal ahead of him. They'd ended the previous day on a high with the cast seemingly quite happy with their performances. No one said it out loud, but it all went more smoothly without Clark. There was a much greater sense of collaboration rather than everyone kowtowing to one big ego.

The only remaining challenge was Minty.

Minty kept shouting 'Cut!' during rehearsal to ask Fletcher about her character's motivation.

'We're not making a film,' Fletcher said patiently and repeatedly. 'Just ask your questions at the break. You're a fairy. A jealous, spiteful being who loves deeply. Just draw from your own life experience.'

Minty had suggested alterations to her lines, her songs and her dance moves. In the end, Fletcher told her that as long as she set the other actors up for their lines, he didn't care what she said or how she said it. He'd put his foot down when it came to the songs.

'I've chosen all of the music very carefully,' he said. 'We don't have time to make those kinds of changes.'

Minty pouted. 'What if we just change my solo at the end? It should be something more uplifting. I'm sure this Billy Eyelash fella is wonderful, but the song doesn't resonate with my character. What about "We'll Meet Again"? There won't be a dry eye in the house.'

'My goal is not to make the audience cry,' Fletcher replied. 'The point is to use contemporary songs. We're sticking with Billie Eyelash... Eilish.'

Then they'd practised with Minty in the harness, being lifted above the cast for the big finale. It was a simple harness, worn under her costume like a jacket with straps around the waist and thighs. Fletcher was hesitant about the stunt, imagining Minty's old bones disintegrating as she was lifted into the air, but Minty was determined.

'I've actually worn something like this before, though under quite different circumstances,' she said, as the rigger adjusted the harness around her bird-like thighs. 'When I was a bit younger.' She winked at the young rigger who blushed right up to his ears.

'You'll be wearing a full skirt for the wedding scene,' Desi said. 'If you waft it about like you're flying, the effect should be enough.'

It was just a matter of hoisting Minty into the air, pausing for applause, then carefully lowering her down again. What could possible go wrong?

Desi was an absolute angel, adapting the costumes for Minty and Fletcher, though it seemed the strain was starting to show. She'd seemed distracted at the rehearsal, had even pricked her finger with a needle, which was unheard of. Fletcher had spotted Desi and Minty huddled in a corner with serious expressions more than once. He just hoped Minty wasn't giving her a hard time about any changes to the Tinkerbell costumes.

Fletcher realised he'd forgotten to ask Desi about the baby

blanket the day before. He'd do that at today's rehearsal. He planned to run through the whole show at least once before Minty returned from court. If the rest of the cast were polished and prepared, then they would hopefully be able to accommodate any shenanigans from Minty Morrigan.

The dogs looked up as Fletcher put his mug in the dishwasher and prepared to leave. 'Sorry, loves. You'll have to wait until later.' He was almost out the door when he returned to the kitchen with the dog leads. 'On second thoughts,' he said. 'Why not add to the chaos.'

Fletcher, Bess and George stopped on the edge of the heath in front of Greenway. There was another white police tent out on the grass.

He spotted Detective Armstrong and headed in his direction. 'Another one?' he said as soon as he was in shouting distance.

Armstrong looked up, said something into the phone he held to his ear, then put it away in his coat pocket. 'Looks like it.'

Fletcher pulled the dogs away. They were straining to get closer to the action.

'Another local?' Fletcher said. He'd briefly seen Minty, May and Cass that morning, so he knew they were all safe and sound. If someone else from the panto had been attacked, he'd just give up.

'Not from Blackheath this time,' Armstrong said. He looked pensive. 'If I had to put money on it, I would've said the body in the tent was the perpetrator of the earlier crimes. Terence Silvers. He's got a record. Stalked Clark Wolfe for years. Harassment, threats of violence. Definitely an unbalanced mind. He's the person who reported Louella's attack. Maybe he just picked the wrong person to attack this time. It's a tangled web.'

So Clark hadn't been lying about the stalker after all. Fletcher felt a stab of guilt for not believing him. And now this Terence Silvers had had a taste of his own medicine. Perhaps he'd attacked someone who fought back for a change. But if that was the case, why hadn't he come forward?

Perhaps the killer this time wasn't a *he*. Fletcher got a bad feeling in his stomach.

He spoke to the detective for a few minutes more before the bells of St Julian's started to chime ten o'clock. Fletcher yelped. 'I'm late!' and hurried away with the dogs. His thoughts returned firmly to Neverland.

CHAPTER 36

LET IT SNOW! LET IT SNOW! LET IT SNOW!

A few hours after her escapade on the heath, May exited a black cab in front of the courthouse, then walked around to the other side of the car to haul Minty out. She still hadn't spoken to Minty about the knife. They hadn't had a moment alone that morning and the taxi driver had been far too chatty for a private conversation.

May's eyes felt sandy from the lack of sleep, her body jumpy with adrenaline as she waited to see if Cass's idea had worked. There was a white tent on the heath, surrounded by SOCO when they'd left Greenway that morning. It was just a matter of time.

And then there was Cass's cancer to think about. When was May's last mammogram?

And the possibility of another Morrigan somewhere in the world. She needed to get the rest of the story from Cass. If they could find her baby, then Greenway might stay in the family.

Hopefully, the hearing wouldn't take long and May would be able to crawl back into her comfy bed to get some sleep so she could think through everything more clearly. She realised that the divorce was the least of her concerns.

May and Minty stood on the pavement side by side. Minty

wore a green dress under her usual layers of cardigan and scarf, all bundled up beneath her best wig which she carefully adjusted as they walked towards the big double doors. May had opted for something plain and simple; comfortable black trousers, a soft white blouse and her trusty old trench coat. She wore one of her favourite Tatty Devine necklaces, laser-cut acrylic in the shape of belladonna flowers. It seemed appropriate to wear the image of a highly poisonous plant to this meeting.

Inside, the courthouse had been perfunctorily decorated for Christmas with tinsel taped in uneven swathes across the front of the reception desk. May and Minty were politely directed to an ancient lift at the end of a dim corridor. 'I'm afraid you're in the older part of the building this morning, fourth floor. Might want to keep your coats on, the heating is a bit patchy up there. Looks like you've got Judge Ellis today,' the clerk said, peering at the computer screen. She adjusted her M&S suit, looked kindly at May and leant forwards. 'Mind your P's and Q's with Ellis. He's a stickler for the formalities. It's always "Your Honour", never "Judge". No swearing, no slang, no chewing gum in Ellis's court.' She gave them a wink as May and Minty shuffled away to meet their fate.

The old, wood-panelled lift was tiny. May and Minty squeezed inside, then awkwardly turned to push the number four button.

'Maximum capacity five people, my arse,' Minty said, pointing to the sign above the doors. 'You'd have to top and tail them like sardines just to fit them in.'

May took a deep breath and let it out slowly. The lift creaked upwards, making unsettling grinding noises along the way. 'We need to talk about the knife at some point,' she said.

'What knife?' Minty's eyes were glued to the display counting down the floors.

'The knife you gave me. The one you said was used to kill Clark.'

'Oh yes,' Minty said. 'That knife. What about it?'

'I don't have it anymore and I'd like to know why you had it in the first place.' Minty wasn't making this easy.

Minty looked at May. 'You got rid of it? Well done. If it's gone, then we can pretend it never existed. And that's all I'm going to say on the matter.'

The lift stopped abruptly and the doors slid open. 'But... why?' May asked as Minty stepped out of the lift and walked away. May stood in the lift so long, dumbfounded by Minty's reaction, that the doors started to close again. She reached out a hand to stop them, then followed after her mother.

May's solicitor was waiting for them, perched on a hard vinyl sofa just outside the doors to the room where they would have the hearing. He stood to kiss each of them on the cheek.

'May, Minty, lovely to see you both. I just wish it was under happier circumstances.' Norman Jolly was the son of one of the St Julian's church volunteers. May had known him since he was a chubby little thing with a habit of eating his own bogeys when he thought no one was looking. He'd grown into a chubby big thing and no longer ate his bogeys, or was just better at hiding it.

'Hello, Norman,' May said. 'Thank you so much for coming today. How long do you think this is going to take?'

Norman laughed. 'We've got Ellis, which is a good thing. The man doesn't suffer fools. We'll be in and out before you can say "contempt of court".'

The old lift began to screech before the doors opened again and James Faraday stepped out. It was the first time May had laid eyes on the man since he'd walked out of Greenway over two years before. He looked older, thinner. Diminished. Probably on some fad diet or a "life-changing" exercise routine. His flesh sagged on his bones, throwing the bags under his eyes into high relief. May could tell that he thought he looked fantastic. That was James all over, typically delusional. He still had the twitchy left eyelid, the one over his glass eye, that belied the usual swagger.

James strode forwards, all confidence, hand extended. 'May, it's good to see you.'

She looked down at his hand, then turned towards her solicitor. 'James, I believe you know Norman Jolly from church.'

James was representing himself. Well, of course he was. May wondered how many solicitors he'd fired before deciding their years of education and experience were useless compared to his own outstanding common sense. At least his arrogance would mean a quick decision. Norman's assessment of Judge Ellis hopefully boded well for them.

James swerved, pretending his hand had always been extended towards Norman. As the two men greeted each other, May became aware of a quiet woman hovering behind James wearing an ill-fitting shift dress and what appeared to be very uncomfortable high-heeled shoes. It was The Other Woman, Gwen Milquetoast. May recognised her from her social media photos.

When James first left, May had spent weeks obsessing over the woman and son he'd kept secret from her for decades. She scoured the internet for information, sifting through the social media of Gwen's friends and family members for data. In photos, Gwen looked younger, more confident. Her posts had evidently been carefully curated and well-edited. In person, the effect was more obviously laborious. The make-up, the nails, the heavily logoed handbag, and shoes that weren't quite right for her outfit belied her working-class background and the shame she felt about it. The fidgeting hands and shifting eyes that returned to James again and again, as if assuring herself that he was still there. The woman was a bag of nerves. She was trying very hard to look haughty and unbothered in May's presence. It was a heroic effort, but futile.

May was sorely tempted to shout 'Boo!' right in her overly made-up face, just to see what would happen.

James was busy doing his obsequious act. May recognised the unctuous look on his face as he tried to schmooze Norman, who, to his credit, was not buying any of it.

Once James had finished displaying his charisma to Norman, his eyes roamed around for his next victim. They, unfortunately for him, fell on Minty.

'Hello, James,' Minty said with a warm smile. 'How's your arsehole?'

Gwen sucked in breath.

'Oh, I wasn't referring to you, dear,' Minty said. She turned back to James. 'Still shitting yourself?'

James remained silent, staring at Minty with a look of fury, spots of high colour on each cheek.

'No?' she continued. 'Well, that's a blessing for you both, isn't it?' She nodded at James and Gwen knowingly just as the courtroom doors opened and their names were called.

As they collected their things and turned to enter the court, May dug through her Kelly bag until she found a pack of peppermint chewing gum, slightly gritty with the sediment at the bottom. She dusted it off, turned and offered it to James. 'Gum?' she asked.

'Your mother needs a muzzle,' he growled, swiping the packet out of May's hand. 'I don't know why she's here at all.'

'Have you forgotten?' May replied. 'Minty is the legal owner of Greenway. It was necessary for her to be here.'

James shook his head, sighed, then popped a piece of gum in his mouth before striding through the doors ahead of everyone else.

Norman caught May's eye. 'Naughty,' he said with a grin, then offered his arm to Minty. The three of them walked in together, leaving Gwen to trail behind.

CHAPTER 37

LAST CHRISTMAS

Fletcher was delighted when the cast made it through the whole show smoothly before Minty's arrival. Bess and George had been an inspired addition as Wendy's dogs. Fletcher kept them happy with bits of cheese from his sandwich, their favourite treat. They behaved beautifully as they always (sometimes) did. The audience would adore them.

He congratulated everyone on the performance and called a break before another run-through. It was a semi-dress rehearsal. Fletcher was performing in the big hoops he would wear under his dresses as Widow Twankey. They affected the way he moved about the stage. He wanted to get used to them before the show. Minty would wear the harness under her clothing when she arrived for the same reason. Fletcher didn't want any surprises.

Desi sat on a chair in front of the stage, methodically snipping seams with a tiny pair of scissors.

'Desi, you're a star doing all this extra work for us,' he said, slipping off the hoops so he could take a seat beside her.

'It's better than decaying away over at Dementia Gardens,' she said.

'I just hope I'm not asking too much. Do say if you need a

break.' He grabbed a water bottle out of the bag at his feet and took a long drink. 'Can I get you anything? A drink? A snack?'

Desi motioned to the thermos tucked into her sewing kit. 'I'm sorted, my dear.'

'I almost forgot,' Fletcher said, fishing his phone out of his bag. 'I wonder if you could take a look at something for me.' He scrolled to the photograph of Caspar's baby blanket then held the phone up for Desi.

Desi adjusted her glasses and leant towards the screen. 'I'm not sure what I'm asking for,' Fletcher explained. 'We're trying to trace the original owner of this baby blanket. I just thought, with your knowledge of fabrics, you might give us some insight.'

Desi stared at the screen so long that Fletcher started to worry she'd forgotten he was there. Just kill him before he got to that age.

'Desi,' he prodded gently. 'What do you make of it?'

'What do you want to know?' she asked quietly.

Fletcher turned his phone to look at the photo. 'Bastian says the fabrics are mostly Georgian designs but could be reproductions. Can you tell the difference?'

'Not original Georgian,' she said. 'The colours are too bright and even. Definitely synthetic colours. I would say that it's decades old, not centuries. Who does it belong to?'

'Jocasta Campbell has it. It was her husband Caspar's when he was a baby, the man who was stabbed on the heath.'

Desi nodded slowly. 'May I see it again?' She took his phone. 'Caspar's. Yes, that makes sense.'

'Does it?' Fletcher asked.

'Poor child,' she said. She looked as if she might cry.

'Desi, are you okay?' Fletcher was overcome with guilt. He shouldn't have bothered Desi with this. She was in her eighties, she was working too hard. He *was* asking too much from her. Then he noticed the dark trail of blood on the fabric in her lap. 'Desi, you've cut yourself!'

She seemed to shake herself out of a dream. 'There're plasters in my sewing kit. I'm sure it's just a nick.'

Fletcher found the first aid kit in her bag, then knelt in front of her to clean and bandage the cut on her hand. Desi continued to stare at the image of the blanket, eyebrows drawn together.

Poor Desi. Fletcher should've been more considerate. May had said that Desi had a daughter who died when she was young. She'd been a budding costume designer like Desi, but had died suddenly. When one loses someone they love so very much, all other deaths prod that grief. It's a wound that never fully heals.

He did his best to clean Desi's hand using the small sterile wipe from the kit, but the blood had collected under the jewellery she wore. It was as he was swiping her fingers that he saw the little ring.

'You wear a Claddagh,' he said. It wasn't surprising he hadn't noticed it before as it was clustered on one finger with three other rings. It looked very much like the one he'd seen in the photo.

Desi looked at her hand. 'It was Dido's,' she said quietly. 'She left it for me when she…' Desi started putting her materials back into the sewing bag. 'Thank you, Fletcher. I think maybe I've been doing a bit too much after all. I'll go home now and lie down for a bit.'

'Of course,' Fletcher said, standing up with her. 'Shall I walk you back? I can carry your bag.'

'No, I'll leave it here for now,' Desi replied as she headed for the door. 'I'd like to be alone. Thank you.'

Fletcher watched helplessly as Desi left the theatre. His own worries seemed suddenly insignificant. He'd been fortunate to never lose anyone that he'd loved deeply, but then there were so few people whom he truly cared about. His thoughts turned to Sparks. Was it too late to join him in Chennai? What if Fletcher spent Christmas with May, then left on Boxing Day? He and Sparks could ring in the new year together.

Why hadn't he thought of this before? It was the perfect plan.

Fletcher clapped his hands to get everyone's attention. 'Shall we try it again from the beginning?'

He took his place at the side of the stage with a new bounce in his step. All being well, he would have his arms around his love by the end of the week.

CHAPTER 38

HAPPY XMAS (WAR IS OVER)

Twenty minutes after entering the courtroom, they were out again. Judge Ellis had castigated James for wasting the court's time, stating that any decent solicitor would have told him he had no claim to Greenway. This, no doubt, was the reason he'd fired each of them. The house legally belonged to Mrs Araminta Morrigan who had generously allowed James to live there rent-free for thirty years. If anything, he owed Mrs Morrigan compensation for the time he'd spent there.

Minty gave an award-winning performance as the angelic, put-upon mother-in-law, eschewing any need for recompense. James actually squirmed in his seat and May left the courtroom exultant as an empress.

At the end of the session, May realised that Gwen hadn't said a word. Her only contribution had been a constant muted clicking as she attempted to surreptitiously pick at her finger-nails. As they stood to leave, May noticed that Gwen's left hand was almost free from the dark varnish she'd been wearing when they'd entered the room. Christ, if that sort of deference was what James wanted, it was no wonder he'd left May. The puzzle was why he'd stayed with her as long as he did.

May, Minty and Norman were the first ones out of the court-room and headed for the lift. May suggested that Minty and Norman go ahead, she would use the loo and meet Minty in the lobby downstairs. The thought of the three of them crammed together inside the tiny lift was more than May could bear.

She found the ladies' room, went into a stall, locked the door, and sat on the closed toilet. May leant forwards, head in her hands. She took a deep breath and let it out slowly.

Thank fuck that was all over with. She took a few more deep breaths, used the loo since she was there, then slowly washed her hands at the sink. She could finally, officially let go of James Faraday. She imagined releasing her grip and watching him fall over a dark precipice, tumbling away into the gloom until she couldn't see him at all. Only hear his increasingly muted screams.

He had no further claim on May or her life. For the first time, she was relieved they'd never had children. A family would've tied them together forever. Now, she never had to see the man again and she was glad of it.

May looked at her reflection in the old mirror over the sink. Time to move forwards and get on with her life. She'd start with Christmas. Minty, May, Fletcher, Cass. Perhaps she'd invite Bastian and some other friends as well. Maybe a proper party. She smiled. May had her lovely home, her dear friends, her complicated family, her hard-won autonomy. She didn't need any more than that. Everything was going to be fine.

Back in the empty corridor, she pushed the button to call the lift and waited. Fletcher would still be at the theatre, but perhaps they could meet for a late lunch. There would certainly be champagne with dinner that evening. Seeing James again had been just what she'd needed. It had reminded May that she wasn't losing anything worth keeping. She was so much better off without him.

May stepped into the lift, feeling lighter than she'd felt in years. The doors had almost shut when a hand inserted itself, forcing them open again. James Faraday stepped inside. His cologne seemed to fill the space around May. She had a brief flash of what it had been like having sex with him, causing her to shudder in disgust.

'May, I'm glad we have a moment to talk *à deux*,' he said, ignoring her repulsed expression. She looked behind him. Where was Gwen? Had he been waiting in the corridor to catch May alone?

'I just wanted to say,' he persisted as the doors closed, 'that I truly hope we can remain close and continue to be good friends.' This was James all over, living in some delusion that suited his prevailing narrative. It could all change at the drop of a hat, depending on what best supported his inflated ego or who was influencing him at the time. The man utterly lacked a sense of self. 'It's a shame this process has tainted the years we spent together,' he continued, 'but I don't for one moment regret our marriage. I don't hate you, May. I hope you know that. I don't hate you.' What possible reason could *he* have to hate her? What an unbelievably stupid thing to say. The man was a moron.

He really had rewritten the past, absolving himself of any wrongdoing in the process, and was projecting an idyllic future that bore no resemblance to their reality. If he just pretended like none of it had happened, then it would be erased. If he acted like May had somehow been the baddie, it would eventually be true. As if she would ever be able to forgive and forget over twenty years of deceit. As if she'd ever forget the way he'd behaved throughout the divorce; the lies he'd told, the way he'd demeaned and belittled her.

She turned her head to look him in the eye for the first time. He was giving her his most earnest puppy eyes and sappy smile. It had, at one time, been one of his more endearing expressions, but that was a long time ago.

'Go fuck yourself,' she said.

James recoiled as if she'd slapped him. 'There's no need to be vulgar,' he replied, pursing his lips into the all too familiar cat's bum and looking down his nose at her. May Morrigan decided there and then that it would be the very last time that James Faraday looked at her that way. She was going to wipe the expression right off his smug face.

Even in that tight compartment, May managed to rear back and land a solid punch square against James's flabby cheek. She put forty years of resentment behind it, the force of which caused his head to ricochet satisfyingly off the opposite wall. His false eye popped out and pinged off the lift doors. The look of shock on his face as he fell was beyond satisfying.

James crumpled at her feet in a heap just as the lift groaned to a halt. May rubbed the knuckles on her right hand. 'You delusional arse,' she said. 'You're not my friend and you never were. I don't know why I put up with you as long as I did. Don't come near me or my home ever again, or I will gut you and feed you to the dachshunds.'

James tried to stand as the lift doors slid open. May stepped over him, ensuring that her right knee connected with his temple, bouncing his head off the side of the lift again. 'Oh, thank goodness,' she said to the couple waiting. 'I'm afraid he's fainted. Poor thing was never any good in a tight space.'

CHAPTER 39

CHRISTMAS WRAPPING

'I can't believe you punched him,' Fletcher said as he popped a cork and started filling glasses. 'I'm surprised he didn't go to the police.'

May took a glass with her left hand, shaking her head. Her right hand rested under an ice pack, the knuckles swollen and sore. 'That would take far too much initiative. And the police would ask a lot of impertinent questions, which would be far too revealing. James prefers his own narrative. Besides, he loves to play the victim. You could say I've given him a parting gift. He can genuinely feel very sorry for himself and have poor Gwen fawning over him for months.'

'He really knows how to push your buttons,' Fletcher said. 'Apart from one. There's one button of yours James Faraday could never find.' He gave a mischievous wink as May laughed.

'You are naughty,' she said. 'But unfortunately correct. Poor Gwen will be enduring his awkwardness now.'

'I never understood what you saw in the man,' Cass replied, taking a glass of champagne. Fletcher restrained himself from raising his eyebrows at this uncharacteristic break in her strict regime. 'He was always so insincere. I can only imagine that particular character trait grew worse over time.'

May sighed. 'You would be right about that.'

The dogs jumped up from their place beside the Aga just before the doorbell rang.

'That'll be Bastian,' May said. 'I invited him round to celebrate with us.'

How delightful. It was turning into a proper party. Fletcher and Bastian could tell May what they'd learnt about the baby blanket, then he'd tell her about his plans to visit Sparks for New Year.

'Hello, hello,' Bastian said as he hung his coat up on the lower hooks May had installed just for him. He kissed her on the cheek. 'I'm guessing from your smile that it's good news, Ms Morrigan? Not that I ever doubted you would triumph.'

'We're moving to the library,' Fletcher said, pushing the drinks trolley in front of him. It was loaded with bottles, a bucket of ice and a bowl of Twiglets. 'More Christmassy there.' Minty tottered behind him holding a Twiglet like a cigarette and nibbling on one end. Somehow, Minty made it look elegant.

May only bought Twiglets at Christmastime. Like the pickled walnuts and the Stilton, some things just taste of Christmas. Though they'd decided to skip the mince pies after what had happened earlier that year. Fletcher shivered at the memory.

The friends gathered around a low table, taking seats in a rough circle made up of a squashy loveseat and four wingback chairs.

'A toast,' Bastian said, raising his glass. He turned to May. 'To divorce, which is not the failure of love, but the determination not to live without it.' Leave it to Bastian to say just the right thing.

'Here, here,' everyone chorused.

'I'd like to make a toast,' Minty said.

Here we go.

Minty held her glass in the air. ''Tis better to have loved and lost, than to put up with the bastard for the rest of your life.'

Everyone drank to that.

'I heard someone got walloped at the crown court this morning,' Bastian said.

'Where did you hear that?' May asked. The Blackheath grapevine was swift, but the courthouse was way over in Bermondsey.

'Darcy Cooper's mother's best friend's sister is the clerk at the reception desk. Said there was a fuss over whether an ambulance was needed or not.' He grinned. Bastian had met James enough times to find this news very funny indeed.

May rolled her eyes. 'For God's sake, the man has no shame. I barely touched him.'

'Now that that's all done and dusted, you can focus on your new lover-man,' Minty said with a wicked grin.

May shook her head. 'I finished with Asa. That relationship has run its course.'

'I can't believe you didn't tell me.' Fletcher was distraught. How could she keep such a thing from him? He'd kept her abreast of all his love affairs in the past. Usually with blow-by-blow accounts, so to speak.

'That's not the lover-man I was talking about,' Minty said, winking at May.

Fletcher's head swivelled between the two of them as Cass chuckled. 'What's this? What have I missed?' he said. Not only had she ended things with Asa, but there was already someone else on the scene! May was never going to hear the end of it.

'I'll tell you later,' May replied, patting his knee. She turned to Bastian, who was also grinning. 'Any news on this latest stabbing? I'm assuming that's what happened. I saw the tent this morning.'

'Yes,' Bastian said. 'Another one. There was a fair bit of excitement this morning. I believe it was a man again, but that's all I know.'

'I spoke to the detective on my way to rehearsal,' Fletcher said as he grabbed a handful of Twiglets. 'He says the man who was killed was called Terence Silvers. He was Clark's stalker. Used to stalk John Cleese but switched to Clark a few years ago, better access. He was probably behind the previous attacks.'

'Then who stabbed *him*?' Bastian asked.

Fletcher shrugged. 'Armstrong said they would see what forensics had to say about it. There were two knives at the scene, one in the attacker's hand and one left in the wound.'

Bastian rubbed his chin. 'But Louella said that Clark attacked her. Is the idea that this guy killed Caspar and Clark, but Clark is the one who attacked Louella? And then someone else killed the killer?' He shook his head. 'It's awfully messy.'

'We should celebrate,' Minty piped up.

'What are we celebrating?' Cass asked.

'Your sister's divorce,' Minty replied, looking nonplussed at Cass's insensitivity.

'Isn't that what we're doing right now?' Cass replied, holding up her glass of champagne.

'We should have a proper celebration,' Minty said, getting into the idea. 'Drinks and nibbles in the library, invite the whole village.'

'I'm not opposed to the idea,' May said. 'In the new year?'

'No,' Minty said. 'Tomorrow night. We'll strike while the iron's hot.'

'What?!' Fletcher yelped. 'Two days before Christmas? The day before the panto? Impossible. I don't have time to organise a party at such short notice.'

'You won't have to lift a finger,' Minty said. 'Cass and I will see to everything.'

Cass choked on her champagne.

'You just invite everyone you know. We'll do the rest.' It seemed Minty had made up her mind.

May gave Fletcher a desperate look, but what could he possibly do?

CHAPTER 40

HAVE YOURSELF A MERRY LITTLE CHRISTMAS

*B*loody Minty and her bloody drinks party. Organising an event two days before Christmas was not an easy job. Cass drove May's ancient Land Rover to the off-licence to collect crates of champagne and then to the supermarket for canapé ingredients. This was after her attempts to find a last-minute caterer had proved fruitless.

At least the fuss on the heath had calmed down. The tent and the police presence were gone. From what Fletcher had said the night before, it seemed her plan was working.

Minty had lost interest in the party almost immediately. She was too wrapped up in rehearsing for the panto, locked in her bedroom wearing enormous headphones to learn all her songs in time. The pop music Fletcher had chosen was a big departure from Minty's usual jazz and big band tunes, but that didn't seem to deter her.

Cass had considered dropping the whole party idea but astonished herself by deciding to persevere. A gathering might be nice. She'd never celebrated the news of her remission. Perhaps, at least in her own mind, the party could be a double celebration.

Like May, Cass had never been much of a cook. She'd scoured

through May's library that morning for menu ideas and, after discarding Mrs Beeton's and something called *Modern Cookery for Private Families* as too fiddly, she'd found a Nigella Lawson cookbook. After scanning the pages, she decided to make mini-Christmas-pudding bonbons and a dip called Roquamole which consisted mostly of avocados and blue cheese. They were both easy to throw together and didn't involve any actual cooking. The rest of the spread would be made up of mini-sausages, crudités for the dip, posh crisps, spicy olives, Christmassy chocolates and anything else that caught her eye.

Cass was surprised how much she was enjoying herself as she loaded her trolley with delicious treats.

'Ms Morrigan?'

She turned around to see the dishy detective standing in the aisle, a packaged sandwich in one hand and a can of drink in the other. He gave her a quizzical look.

'Hello,' she said. Christ, what was his name?

'Planning a party?' He nodded at the trolley.

'Yes,' Cass said. 'It's tonight at the house. Very last-minute. Just drinks and nibbles. You should come.' She dialled down her trans-Atlantic accent and dialled up the English to sound more like May.

'I'm not sure...' he said, still staring at her intently, eyes drawn together creating a deep crease between them.

'Most of the village will be there,' she said. 'You can consider it part of your investigation into the stabbings.'

'Well, perhaps.'

'I'd really like for you to come,' she said, looking into his eyes, seeing his pupils dilate. That had done the trick. He *wanted* to believe she was May. He would be there. 'Must dash,' Cass said, turning to go. Her mantra was to always leave them wanting more. 'See you this evening.'

She walked towards the tills, humming to herself. The party was going to be even more fun than she'd anticipated.

CHAPTER 41

ROCKIN' AROUND THE CHRISTMAS TREE

May wasn't in the mood for a party. She sat at the kitchen table, weighed down with worry about Cass's health, the child she'd had, the knife Minty had given May and what it all meant. Anxiety had been swirling through her body all morning. Her right hand still ached from slugging James the day before.

She needed Fletcher, but he was out of the house before May was even up. The panto would fill his time right up to Christmas Day. She would have to deal with these things on her own.

It was nice of Minty to suggest a party. May had been surprised when Cass agreed to organise it, but May was tired. Her previous day in court had marked the end of a long, emotional journey that started two years before when James walked out.

No, that wasn't quite true. It had begun two years before that, when he'd been diagnosed with cancer. Four years of turmoil and upheaval. Four years of worry, stress, obliteration and regeneration. Strangely enough, the healing had been the hardest part. When things were at their worst, there was little May could do except survive. It was in the periods of calm that the real work happened. Those were the moments when she would drag herself out of the depths, look around and see what was left of her life.

Finally, she'd reached a place of safety. She'd built new emotional foundations, reconnected with her body and spirit, and dealt with James and his toxicity for the very last time. Now, all she wanted to do was rest.

I can do whatever I want.

Her Christmas shopping was done. The dogs were walked and fed. Fletcher and Minty were at the panto rehearsals. Cass was out buying things for the party. No one would care if she took the day off.

She picked up her phone and sent one text message:

Festive drinks at mine from 8. Tell everyone.

Darcy Cooper would do the rest.
May Morrigan went back to bed.

When May stepped out of the shower hours later, she could hear voices downstairs, what sounded like furniture being moved, and the occasional burst of music. While showering, she'd carefully checked both breasts for lumps, feeling light-headed with fear the whole time. Thankfully, she'd found nothing sinister.

May was tempted to go down to supervise the pre-party chaos, but stopped herself. She hadn't asked for the party. Minty had offered to throw the event in honour of May's divorce. They were perfectly capable of sorting it out without her.

She took her time getting dressed, drying then straightening her hair into a razor-sharp bob. She carefully applied light make-up with a fierce red lipstick. After spritzing herself with *Le Baiser du Dragon* (a vintage bottle purchased before the dreadful refor-mulation), she dressed in the metallic-gold trouser suit she'd been saving for a special occasion. Just as the party was due to start, May headed for the stairs.

The dogs greeted her with enthusiasm. Someone had put them in their Christmas jumpers and they looked particularly adorable. The library was glowing with a blazing fire, the tree was twinkling and May's desk had been turned into a temporary bar with bottles of fizz in a big bucket of ice and sparkling glasses lined up beside it. Christmas music played from the speakers overhead. Cass and Minty had done well.

'Oh, for God's sake,' Cass said from behind her.

May turned to see Cass standing in the doorway carrying a platter of crudités. She was wearing a metallic-gold trouser suit. 'You've got to be joking,' May said. 'You'll have to change.'

'I'm not changing,' Cass replied. 'I've got nothing to change into. These are the only party clothes I packed.' She set the platter on a low table.

'I'm not changing,' May said. 'It's *my* party.'

Minty toddled in wearing her red velvet dress and carrying a martini. She looked from one daughter to the other and chuckled. 'It's like when you were young and insisted on dressing the same. You looked just as stupid then as you do now.' She settled into a chair by the fire.

'Thanks for your input,' May said to Minty, then turned back to Cass. 'You can wear something of mine. Choose whatever you like.'

Cass looked May up and down. 'The suits aren't exactly the same,' she said. 'It's not that big a deal. I'm not going to change.'

'But–' May felt suddenly furious.

'Happy Christmas!' Fletcher threw his arms in the air as he made his entrance wearing a metallic-gold trouser suit. He looked from Cass to May, then dropped his arms. 'Oh. Well, this is awkward.'

Minty chewed on an olive. 'Apparently, I didn't get the memo.'

'Fuck's sake,' May said.

The doorbell rang. The party had begun.

The library was soon bustling with friends, old and new. Darcy had done her job well. Danny Fox, a young writer, was there with his partner, Suzy. His first book was being published in the new year, so they were in high spirits. May wondered if a wedding might be in their near future. Suzy's sister, Chloe, was home from Trinity College, Cambridge, full of stories about matriculation, the Great Court Run, Formal Halls and punting on the Cam. Chloe and Minty hit it off immediately. The two of them spent much of the evening huddled together, giggling by the fire.

May's cleaner, Jilly, arrived with her partner Muriel. Muriel was the village florist. She presented May with a huge Christmas bouquet of red roses, thistle, holly and willow. Father David brought his new manservant, Paolo. Cass floated around the room from one group to another, topping up glasses with a festive cocktail she'd discovered in one of May's cookbooks. Fletcher was surrounded by the panto company, animatedly sharing stories, waving his glossy nails about as he spoke. The party spilt out into the entry hall, so full was May's library with the great and good of Blackheath.

Harold Lambert had come with his granddaughter, Tansy. 'Thought a little festive cheer would do us both some good,' he said. Jocasta had chosen to stay home and rest, and who could blame her. May spotted Desi sitting on a little sofa with Tansy and Bastian. They seemed to be entertaining the little girl with a story. Bastian was making funny faces as Desi and Tansy laughed. Bastian was always good with children. The sight of them made May think of Desi's daughter, Dido. She'd had ginger hair like Tansy's, though Dido's had been much more vibrant. What must it be like to lose a child? Dido, Caspar, Cass's unknown baby. So much loss.

May stood at the door to her library, drinking in the sight of her friends and family all gathered together in her home. Only two years before, she'd stood at that very same spot, lost and bereft, with the empty house echoing around her, her future a frightening ellipsis. Time, remarkable friends, and a lot of hard work had got her through it.

'Hello, lovely lady.' Asa stood beside her, drink in hand.

May looked around. 'No Margaret?' she asked.

'She may be here,' he said with a grin. 'But she's not with me this evening.'

May just smiled in reply.

Asa looked up. 'No mistletoe, now that's a pity.'

May kissed him on one cheek, then patted the other cheek with her hand. 'Go find Margaret,' she said before moving away to mingle.

She was talking to Jean Drysdale when she spotted DCI Armstrong on the other side of the room. He'd arrived with a bottle of Veuve Clicquot (very nice) and was handing it to Cass. May caught his eye and saw him do a double-take, looking from Cass to May then back again. When Cass walked away to put the bottle on ice, he headed in May's direction.

'You didn't know there were two of us,' she said.

'What a terrifying thought,' Armstrong replied. 'I now realise it was your sister who invited me this morning. I hope you don't mind.' He gestured at May's outfit. 'Is this some kind of Greenway uniform? I noticed Dr Redmond dressed the same.'

May laughed. 'Cass, Fletcher and I seem to have the same taste in party outfits.'

'Any news about the stabbings?' Jean asked. She often walked on the heath with her dog, Tarquin.

Armstrong sighed. 'It looks like the last person killed was the perpetrator of the previous crimes. We're still working on who stabbed him.'

'Does this put an end to the attacks?' Jean said.

'There's no end to crime in this city,' Armstrong said, 'but perhaps it's the end to this particular spate of crimes.'

'That's brilliant news.' Jean waved at someone on the other side of the room. 'I'm going to go tell Sarah.'

Once Jean departed, Armstrong stepped closer to May.

'What makes you think this Terence Silvers was responsible for the other attacks?' she asked quietly.

'Two knives on the scene, one in his hand, one in the wound on his leg. Preliminary forensics suggest the knife in his hand held DNA from Caspar Campbell, Louella Alard and Clark Wolfe. It seems to be the weapon used in those attacks,' he replied.

'But you don't agree?' May watched his face closely.

He grimaced. 'Something's not right about the whole thing,' he said. 'The first two attacks, the victims were stabbed in the stomach. Violent jabs that left bruises around the wounds. Mr Wolfe was stabbed in the heart, almost timidly. Then this guy is slashed across the thigh.' He scratched his nose. 'The same knife might've been used but it wasn't by the same person. I feel it in my water.'

May looked over his shoulder to see Cass watching them intently. May subtly nodded, it seemed Cass's plan had worked, to an extent. She focused back on Armstrong. 'What about Louella saying that Clark attacked her?'

He shrugged. 'None of it makes sense.' His eyes moved across her face as he spoke. From one eye to the other, down to her mouth, then back again. Was he thinking about their kiss? 'If Wolfe attacked Mr Campbell and Miss Alard with the knife, how did Silvers get his hands on it? He was stalking Wolfe, watching him. Was even staying in the same hotel. Maybe Wolfe tried to attack him, but he managed to get hold of the knife and used it against him? I'll get to the bottom of it.'

'And who killed the killer?' she said. 'Any clues, Detective?'

His mouth looked so inviting. They'd never discussed the kiss. Did he regret it? She didn't think so.

He shook his head. 'No clue yet. They must've been wearing gloves. No fingerprints or DNA on the second knife in the wound, except his own.' He took a step back, breaking the tension between them. 'That brings up a curious detail,' he said, looking away from her.

May had been enjoying the tension. Irritated by the detour, she realised he was looking at Minty. 'What detail?' she asked, trying to catch his eye again.

He continued to stare at Minty as he said, 'We found fingerprints on the knife in his hand matched to your mother and Mrs Desdemona Meade. How do you think that happened?'

'How do you know the prints are Minty's and Desi's?' May asked, trying to buy time to think. In May and Cass's haste to plant the knife and get away, they must've forgotten to wipe it. Minty noticed the detective staring at her and wandered over.

'Your mother and Mrs Meade both have their prints on file. Mrs Meade slapped a police constable at a Labour rally in the nineties. Your mother,' he paused to look from Minty to May. 'You really don't know?'

May shook her head.

'There's no need to go into details,' Minty said. 'It was such a long time ago.'

'Last summer your mother was arrested for shoplifting,' he continued. 'At a shop called The Pleasure Chest in Soho.'

'It was all a simple misunderstanding,' Minty quickly interjected. 'That item must've fallen into my bag when I wasn't looking. It apparently caught on something and suddenly inflated as I was leaving the shop. Absolutely terrifying. Thankfully, I was eventually able to calm the situation without involving my daughter.'

May and Armstrong stared at Minty.

'And that's all I'm going to say on the matter,' Minty said, walking away with her head held high.

CHAPTER 42

HURRY SANTA

Fletcher flopped into a chair beside May. His back ached from standing all evening and his new shoes had chafed uncomfortably. He was fairly certain a blister had formed on his right heel. This was the price one paid for gorgeousness.

Every surface in the library was covered with dirty glasses, crumbs and colourful streamers from the party poppers Cass had distributed towards the end of the night. The dogs had put themselves to bed in the kitchen hours before, seeking sanctuary from what had become a somewhat raucous party. Minty sat on the sofa wearing enormous headphones, bobbing her head and mumbling to herself. Her commitment to the panto was admirable.

'Where did Cass get to?' Fletcher asked.

'I think she went to bed,' May replied. 'She did well. It was a good night.' She looked at Fletcher. 'I'm pleased to get you alone. There are a few things I'd like to talk to you about.'

This sounded serious. 'Sure,' he said. 'But I'm so tired, I'm not sure I'll be much use.'

May looked over at Minty. 'Minty, would you like another drink?'

Minty continued to bob and mumble.

'Just making sure she can't hear us,' May said, satisfied. 'All you have to do is listen.' She sat forwards. 'You know the last attack on the heath? That Terence Silvers?' Fletcher nodded; was May going to confess? 'Cass killed him,' she said.

'She what?' Fletcher said. Jesus wept. It must be some kind of genetic flaw in the Morrigan blood. He didn't for one moment doubt that it was true. 'Why did she do that?'

'He tried to attack us. It was purely self-defence,' May replied.

'Did you tell the police this?' Maybe it wasn't as bad as he first imagined.

'No,' May said. 'There's more to it.'

Of course there was.

May rubbed the back of her neck, then turned her head from side to side. There was a crackling sound. 'Minty gave me the knife that was used to stab Clark. I learnt tonight that it was also used to stab Caspar and Louella, I'm assuming by Clark. I'm not sure about that bit though. It's a bit of a muddle. After Cass stabbed this man on the heath, she had the idea of planting the knife on him so that he'd be blamed for the previous attacks.'

'But why?' Fletcher said. It didn't make any sense.

'To draw attention away from Minty,' May said. 'But, we foolishly forgot to wipe the knife for prints so both Minty's and Desi's prints were on it.'

Fletcher's head was spinning. He closed his eyes, trying to sift through the information. He wished he had a pinboard and some note cards. 'Let's back up,' he said, keeping his eyes closed. 'Why did Minty have the knife in the first place?'

'She and Desi found Clark's body. I guess they picked it up then. For some reason, Minty brought it home and gave it to me. She refuses to say any more about it.'

Fletcher opened his eyes. 'That's innocent enough. You could explain it to the police. It wasn't a terribly bright thing to do, but it's not as if Minty stabbed Clark. Or did she? Good God, does homicide actually run in the family?'

May thought it over. 'There's more to it than that. Terence Silvers says he saw Minty and Desi dump Clark's body. He says Minty killed him, but I can't see how Minty or Desi could've killed Clark. He could easily have overpowered them, even if they were working together. No, I think Minty just picked up the knife. But it's complicated by the fact that I put it in my handbag and didn't mention it to Gus. Then Cass and I were attacked and it made sense to get rid of the knife, killing two birds with one stone.'

Fletcher rubbed his eyes. It was after midnight and they still needed to tidy up before going to bed. Tomorrow was Christmas Eve when they'd all attend the village procession, then he had the panto performance. The morning after that was Christmas Day. He still needed to brine the turkey, peel the potatoes, the parsnips, prepare the sprouts, wrap the rest of the gifts. And now this nonsense about Minty and the knife and Cass killing someone on the heath.

'All right,' he looked at May, 'for the sake of sanity, let's just accept the situation as it is, no backsies. Where does that leave us?'

'Gus said that both Minty's and Desi's prints are on the knife,' May said.

'Does that make them suspects?' Fletcher asked.

'I don't think it makes them suspects, but it raises questions,' she said.

'Questions are fine,' he said. 'It's the answers that could cause trouble, and we won't be providing those.' Perhaps May was worried about nothing. As long as they kept their mouths shut, the problem would eventually go away.

'Yes,' May said with a sigh. 'You're right. As long as none of us says anything, there's not an issue.' She seemed to relax a bit.

'Anything else?' Fletcher asked. 'You said there were *a few* things we needed to talk about.'

'Why don't I top up your drink first?' May said.

God, that wasn't a good sign. 'I'll pass on the drink. I'm up early tomorrow,' Fletcher said, bracing himself. 'Go ahead.'

May took a deep breath. 'Cass was treated for breast cancer a few months ago, but was given the all-clear after surgery and chemo. That's why she came home to Blackheath. She fell pregnant when we were all at the Isle of Wight Festival years ago. She had the baby, but I don't know any more than that yet. And I ended things with Asa because he wants to see other people, but I'm not sure what I want yet.'

Fletcher felt like his brain was going to short-circuit with all of this information. 'Anything else?'

'I kissed DCI Armstrong, but I don't know if it meant anything or if he's interested in me or if it was just because I was stoned at the time.'

Fletcher held up a hand to stop the flow of words. 'Give me a moment.' His brain sifted through the new information, attempting to prioritise. 'Cass had cancer? Is she all right now?' Fletcher had lost a number of friends to cancer over the years. Unfortunately, one didn't reach seventy without such tragedies.

'She says she is,' May said. 'It frightened her though. It must be what all the exercise and dieting is about. She stared into the face of her own mortality and realised she wasn't ready to die.'

'But what's the point in living if she's not enjoying her life? Hopefully, she'll loosen up with time. She did have a few glasses of champagne at the party, and I think I saw her eat a chipolata,' he said. Poor Cass. What must it be like to go through something like that? Fletcher never took his own good health for granted. He touched the wooden table beside him.

'I've booked a check-up with my doctor,' May said. 'Just for reassurance.'

Of course. He hadn't considered that May could be at risk

of the same fate. His stomach dropped. 'Yes, you must stay on top of it,' he said. The thought of losing May was devastating. He realised that she looked tired. This news about Cass, Minty's antics, her divorce. It was a lot to be carrying on her own. He'd been so distracted with the panto, he hadn't even noticed. 'I'm sorry, I've had my head up my own backside the last few weeks.'

May reached out and patted his hand. 'You've had a lot on your plate,' she said. 'And I know you're missing Sparks.'

Sparks. Fletcher felt a stab of guilt. He'd been planning to leave May to see Sparks in Chennai for New Year. He wouldn't do that now. She needed him here.

'What's this about Cass having a child?' he said. 'After the Isle of Wight. That's around the same time you...'

May nodded and looked away.

Fletcher had been there for the drama and trauma that came with May's brief pregnancy.

'Did she give the baby up for adoption?' he asked.

'I don't know,' May replied. She leant her head against the wing of her chair. 'She was telling me about it just before we were attacked... then I was in court... then the party.' She closed her eyes. 'She only said she had the baby and gave it up. I don't know the rest.'

He nodded. The story of the child, who would now be over fifty years old, could wait.

'And what about Asa and Armstrong?' he asked quietly.

May smiled without opening her eyes. 'Asa was just what I needed at the time, but now I need something else. What that is has yet to be determined. Gus is... undefined.' She opened her eyes. 'We'll see.'

'Go to bed,' Fletcher said. 'I'll deal with this.' He gestured to the room around him.

'Leave it,' May said as she stood up. 'I'll tidy up tomorrow. You've got the panto to think about.' She stretched and yawned.

'The procession isn't until four, I've got all day to tidy.' She leant down to kiss his forehead. 'Goodnight, Fletch. And thank you.'

'For what?' he asked.

'For sharing the load,' she said as she headed for the door.

Fletcher sat silently, thinking over the things May had told him. He'd forgotten to mention Desi's Claddagh and how it had belonged to her daughter, Dido. Had Dido ever had a baby? Minty snored quietly on the sofa.

He decided to help Minty to bed, do a bit of cleaning, then go to bed himself. He touched Minty's hand. 'Minty,' he said. 'Time for bed.'

Minty snorted herself awake, then looked at him from beneath the false lashes she'd worn for the party. One of them had come unglued at the corner and was stuck to her eyebrow. 'Come on, old girl,' he said, hoisting her up off the sofa.

'I'm fine.' She snatched her arm away. 'Don't "old girl" me. I can sort myself out.' She yawned, causing her dentures to click, then chomped them back into place. 'So, I'm a grandmother after all,' she said, looking at Fletcher.

'What? You were listening?'

'Impossible not to,' Minty replied. 'You two need to learn how to whisper.' She left the library scratching her scalp under the favourite blonde wig.

So, that particular cat was out of the bag. He would need to tell Cass. What else had Minty heard? Probably everything, knowing her.

Fletcher began to collect the dirty glasses, placing them on a tray to carry to the kitchen. He realised that there was still at least one big question remaining: if Clark stabbed Caspar for some unknown reason, then stabbed Louella as she says he did, and Cass stabbed Silvers… then who killed Clark Wolfe?

CHAPTER 43

WINTER WONDERLAND

The Christmas Eve procession was May's favourite night of the year. She'd attended it since she was a child, usually leaving a grumpy James at home to go on her own in more recent years.

One Christmas, when she and Cass were eleven years old, they'd had the honour of playing Mary and Joseph, proudly riding the donkey from the Catholic church at the top of the village down to St Julian's on the heath. May had been precariously perched on its back with a blue scarf draped over her head and a cushion under her dress to mimic a pregnant belly. An eleven-year-old with a baby bump hadn't seemed odd at the time.

Cass had walked beside her, looking sombre, tea towel strapped to her head with one of Minty's belts and a wonky moustache and beard drawn onto her face in marker pen that later, much to May's amusement, turned out to be permanent ink. Cass had spent all of Christmas and New Year trying to scrub the stuff off her increasingly inflamed face.

'It's about to start!' May shouted from the entry hall. Cass and Minty shuffled out of the library as Fletcher came scurrying from the kitchen, smelling of ham and cloves. He'd spent all morning at the little theatre, rushed home to cook, then would return to the theatre after the procession to prepare for the performance. He'd packed himself an enormous ham sandwich to tide him over.

'Is that my Barbara Hulanicki blouse?' May asked, looking at Cass.

'You said I could wear anything of yours,' Cass replied. '"Choose whatever you like" is exactly what you said.'

'I meant for the party,' May replied. 'As you well know. At least it makes a change from that dreadful sportswear you've had on all week.'

'Where are the bloody dog leads!?' Fletcher said. The stress was getting to him.

Finally, they were all wrapped up and ready to set off. The dogs led the way on the hurriedly found leads. It was already dark, the heath lit only by softly glowing lamp-posts dotted beside the pathway. Traffic had been blocked off to allow the procession to take over so that Blackheath sat remarkably peacefully in the golden light. The ghostly shapes of others were visible all over the heath, torchlights bobbing like drunken fireflies, all aiming for the top of the village to wait for Mary and Joseph to appear.

May's group moved at Minty's pace, which was slow-going. People passed them on all sides, many stopping to wish them a happy Christmas. At last, the little gang found a spot in front of the butcher shop. May waved to Nick, the butcher, tidying up behind the counter. The queue for his Christmas turkeys had snaked along the pavement all day. Fletcher, bless him, had been up and out first thing to collect theirs.

'That reminds me,' Cass said, looking at the butcher shop. 'Why is there a turkey in a bucket of water in the kitchen?'

'Fletcher likes to soak the turkey in brine,' May replied. 'Makes it nice and juicy.'

Fletcher winked at them both.

The clomping sound of the donkey's hooves could be heard, causing the crowd to quieten as Father David and the priest appeared with lanterns, leading Mary and Joseph through Blackheath. May recognised the children from St Julian's primary where she volunteered as a reader. They looked proud, but slightly uncomfortable in their robes. Joseph no longer wore a tea towel on his head, only colourful robes. Someone had done their biblical research.

The villagers flooded behind with their torches, filling the street. They walked slowly under the fairy lights, sedate but joyful, creating a magical atmosphere of community and belonging.

May thought about the many times she'd attended the procession as a child. She and Cass would always manage to slip away from their parents and lose themselves in the crowd. It was never frightening because they were surrounded by familiar faces, with the lights of Greenway visible on the opposite side of the heath. The girls always found their way home.

Then there were the teen years, wondering if one boy or another would hold her hand at the carols. The years with James, the years without him, when he stayed home and she went alone. And now she was walking the procession with Cass and Minty again. She would never have guessed that that would happen. And Fletcher too, looking handsome but distracted, his mind on the performance later that evening.

The crowd was met on the steps of St Julian's by a small band for the Christmas carols. The first song was always 'Away in a Manger' and the event ended with 'Silent Night'. It was tradition. No song sheets were needed. Everyone knew the words.

They were halfway through 'God Rest Ye Merry Gentlemen' when May spotted Armstrong moving through the crowd, scanning faces as he went. She slipped to the edge of the gathering and waited.

'Ms Morrigan,' he said when he reached her.

'Do call me May,' she said. 'Are you working?' The muted light on the heath softened his craggy features.

'I'm always working,' he said, then turned to admire the church, lit by floodlights. 'It's a special event. Do you do this every year?'

'For as long as I can remember,' she replied. 'Any news?'

He looked back at her. 'Your mother and Mrs Meade have been cleared of the murder.' He gave a small smile. 'Not that they were ever serious suspects. Silvers was staying at the hotel linked to Demeter Gardens. The knife matches the knives used there and in the care home.' His eyes were doing that searching thing across her face. She'd love to know what was going through his mind. 'I know Mrs Meade lives at Demeter Gardens and I understand your mother has been spending time there. They must've handled the knife at some point before the crimes were committed. The blade was wiped, but the knife itself wasn't properly cleaned between attacks. Cotton fibres were found on the serrated blade, either from clothing or from being wrapped in fabric. We're searching Silver's belongings and his hotel room.'

What had Cass done with the napkin? May hadn't put it back in her bag. Cass must've taken it. 'I guess I should cancel the cake with a file in it that I ordered for Minty,' she said.

'May.' Goosebumps tingled up both arms when he said her name. 'Now that your mother isn't a suspect, I think we should talk about that kiss.'

She raised her chin to look him in the eye. 'Talk?' she said with a small smile. 'That's what you want to do? Talk about it?'

He shook his head as he leant forwards. 'You're right, talking is overrated.'

'My feet are killing me!' Minty was beside May, leaning on Cass's arm. Armstrong took a step back. Damn Minty!

'Why don't you go home and rest up for the panto?' May said. 'Cass will take you home.' She gave Cass the look that said *just do it and don't argue.*

'No,' Minty said. 'I don't want to go all the way home, then come out again. Take me to the theatre. I've got my flask. I'll eat after the show. I can rest there.'

All the way home was less than a hundred metres, but then May wasn't ninety-six. She looked at Cass again.

'I'll take her,' Cass said.

'You don't need to *take* me anywhere,' Minty said with indignation. 'I'm perfectly capable of taking myself, thank you very much.' But she didn't let go of Cass's arm.

'I'm sure you can,' Cass replied. 'But I'd like to walk with you, if I may.'

Minty sighed dramatically. 'If you insist.'

As Cass and Minty ambled off towards the theatre, May turned to resume her conversation with Armstrong, only to find that he was gone.

CHAPTER 44

WHEN A CHILD IS BORN

Cass deposited Minty at the little theatre. Fletcher wasn't thrilled to have Minty there so early, but that wasn't Cass's problem. She slowly made her way back through the village. The street had already been reopened to traffic, though the pavements were still full of families, the pubs and restaurants overflowing. Everyone would eat, then reconvene in the theatre for the panto that evening. Cass was actually looking forward to it. She might even allow herself a bit of the delicious-smelling ham that had been simmering on the Aga all day.

It was odd being back in Blackheath. The familiarity of the village traditions was both comforting and unsettling. It was nice that some things hadn't changed, but she'd been away so long that she couldn't help but feel like an outsider. Things that had made sense in her youth seemed faintly odd now. A pregnant child on a donkey? She'd never really thought about it before. She saw these things through two sets of eyes, both native and foreign. Cass, herself, felt caught between the two.

At Greenway, she found May in the library with a glass of amaretto, staring at the lights of the Christmas tree. 'Cass, come join me,' she said.

They were home alone. It was time to finish their talk.

Cass passed on the drink, but she took the chair across from May. 'It's been a big week. How are you doing?' she asked.

May looked at her. Cass had that old feeling of looking into a mirror. 'I'm not really sure,' May said. 'How are you? Not doing too much?' She took a sip, keeping her eyes on Cass.

Cass shook her head. 'I've got more energy than I did when I first arrived and my appetite is coming back. I think I'm doing okay. Do you want to talk about the baby?' Best to just grab the bull by the horns.

'Yes,' May said. 'But first, what did you do with the napkin that was wrapped around the knife?'

Cass looked at the fire. 'I burnt it,' she said. 'As soon as we got back. Don't tell me you need it?'

'No, that's perfect,' May said with relief. She adjusted herself in the armchair before looking at Cass. 'Tell me what happened,' she said.

Cass sent her mind back to the time she'd spent most of her life avoiding.

'After Jimi died, I lost interest in life. That Christmas I decided to drop out of Cambridge and follow Percy and the Zeppelin to the States. We were just getting home pregnancy tests in England, but it would be years before they were available in the US. Months passed before I finally saw a doctor and had the pregnancy confirmed.' So much of that time had become a blur, but she remembered hours on the tour bus, being constantly hungry, living in caftans to conceal her growing belly.

She was the official tour photographer. Those photographs had been the beginning of her career and formed the basis of her first book, though she'd left out the part about being pregnant at the time. There was one photo she'd never shown anyone. She'd taken it standing in front of a mirror in a hotel room just outside of LA, her stomach an almost perfect sphere clinging to her skinny body. Percy had said she looked like a string with a knot tied in the middle.

'There was nothing I could do except have the baby by then, but I knew I couldn't keep it. I gave birth in Houston. That's why there aren't any photos of that stop on the tour. I went to the hospital when my water broke, had the baby, and was back on the bus the following day. We left Texas as if it had never happened.'

She'd cried every day for weeks afterward. Her body had yearned for that child. Cass developed mastitis when her milk came in and there was no baby to take it. She'd stood under the shower in San Antonio and New Orleans, breasts hot and hard with milk, crying her eyes out as she tried to relieve the pressure. A doctor in Orlando had treated her with contempt about the missing baby as he prescribed antibiotics for the infection. She finally lied, saying the baby had died, which had hurt her more than the truth, but it made the bastard of a doctor treat her with a modicum of kindness.

'What happened to the baby?' May asked.

'Adoption,' Cass said.

'Was it a boy or a girl?'

Cass shrugged. 'I don't know. I never even looked at the child. If I'd known anything about him or her, I wouldn't have been able to let go, and letting go was the best thing for both of us.' She didn't tell May about reaching out right after the birth and, for a brief moment, feeling a tiny hand wrap itself around her finger before the nurses took the baby away. That memory belonged to Cass, and Cass alone.

May reached out and held Cass's hand. 'Cass, I'm so sorry.'

'I had to sign some papers,' Cass continued. 'And that was it. I was a foreign, unmarried mother. They couldn't get rid of me fast enough.'

'And you've never tried to go back and find them?' This seemed to be the most surprising part of it to May. May, who'd always wanted to know everything about everyone, who found it impossible to let anything go.

Cass shook her head. 'I've tried to pretend like it never happened. I've even avoided Texas as much as possible. It was only when you mentioned that Greenway would go to the council that I wondered if…'

'Yes,' May said. 'I wondered the same thing.' She sat back in her chair. 'The child would be in his or her fifties now. You're probably a grandmother, maybe even a great-grandmother if they stayed in Texas.'

'Fuck off,' Cass said.

'I'm serious,' May replied. 'There could be a whole line of Morrigans out there with no idea of their heritage.' She sat forwards and looked Cass in the eye. 'Let's go to Texas.'

'Don't be ridiculous,' Cass said. 'The chances of finding out what happened are slim to none. The files were probably never put onto computers. Where would we even begin?'

'At the hospital,' May said. 'I'll do some research online and we'll go from there. You'll have to be on board though. It will make things go faster if you, as the mother, are involved.'

"The mother". It wasn't a word Cass had ever associated with herself.

'You haven't told me who the father was,' May said. 'Do you know?'

'Of course I know!' Cass replied. 'What kind of woman do you think I am?' This was going to be the hardest part for May to hear. Cass considered lying. Did it matter if the truth ever came out?

'Well?' May persisted. 'Who was it?' May would find out the truth, one way or another.

Cass swallowed hard before answering. She looked May in the eye, knowing that what she was about to say would change everything. 'It was James. James Faraday, your ex-husband is the father of my child.'

CHAPTER 45

SANTA BABY

Fletcher peered at his reflection in the warped loo mirror as he made up his face for the panto. He stood by the open window, relishing the rush of cold air. For some reason, the theatre was boiling and he didn't want his make-up to melt before they'd even started.

It had been months since he'd done a full face, but they were skills one didn't forget. Of course, the Dame's cartoonish visage was very different to the tasteful style of Fletcher's former alter ego, Barbara Bouvier. Barb's passing, months before, had been a cathartic moment, ushering in a new age for Fletcher. His two personas had become one.

Barb had been born when he'd last played Widow Twankey during his time at Cambridge. Putting on the dress and wig back then had triggered something within himself, something he couldn't resist. He'd spent decades living as both Barb and Fletch. Now, he was learning how to meld those two wonderful beings into one fabulous self.

He'd not told May, but part of his reluctance to play the Dame was wondering how he would feel back in that role. Would he miss Barb? Would he regret the changes he'd made?

It was with relief that he could answer definitively that he had no desire to return to his previous existence. He loved Barb. He always would. A special kind of nostalgia surrounded all memories of her, but he would never be her again. And that was fine.

'Why is it so hot?' Minty barged into the men's loos, half-dressed in her costume. 'I'm not wearing the tights. I'll die from heat exhaustion.'

'Fine. Whatever,' Fletcher said. 'I've spoken to Cecil about the heating. He said he'll see to it.' Two more hours and it would all be over. They'd rehearsed their hearts out. It was in the hands of the panto gods now. Two hours, and Fletcher would have his life back.

May and Cass knocked on the door, then popped their heads in.

'Are you decent?' Cass asked.

'Never, darling,' Fletcher replied in his Widow Twankey voice.

Cass laughed, but May looked dazed and remained unusually silent. Had she been at the gummies again?

'Are you all right, love?' he asked.

May pasted on a smile. 'Yes, of course. It's just sweltering in here. We should've brought you a fan.' She looked him up and down. 'Is this the birth of a new Barb?'

'Nope,' he said firmly. 'It's all me, sweetheart. All one glorious me.'

The hall filled quickly with standing room only at the back. May, Cass and Bastian had snagged seats on the front row. Bastian set up an iPad on the seat beside him so even Louella could watch from her hospital bed.

The troupe gathered behind the stage for Fletcher's pre-show pep talk. 'You've all worked hard for this,' he said, looking from face to face. Desi was still stitching at the longer hem on Minty's costume. 'We've had quite a few obstacles along the way, but we've created something special together. It's not going to be perfect, but it's going to be memorable.'

'Has someone sorted out the heat?' Minty interrupted. 'I'm roasting in this get-up.'

'Yes,' Fletcher said. 'Cecil says he's turned it right off for the time being.' He looked at Cecil who nodded agreement. 'Anyone else have any questions?' He'd completely lost his train of thought after Minty butted in, so he just wrapped things up by saying, 'Fuck it, darlings. Let's make 'em laugh.'

The group whooped their approval. Bess and George, in the arms of their Wendy, barked with excitement. It was time to start the show.

Apart from a few minor snags and a lot of improvisation whenever Minty was onstage, the play went remarkably smoothly. The audience laughed when they were supposed to, sang along when encouraged, and participated in the jokes and traditional banter. Fletcher spotted Tansy Campbell, on Harold's knee, laughing and clapping her hands to the music as he bobbed her up and down.

DCI Armstrong was there, hovering in the background, but Fletcher saw him mouthing the words to more than one song during the show.

Then it was time for the grand finale and Minty's solo. It was almost over. She stepped into the spotlight, nodding to Cecil, who was in charge of the backing tracks. To Fletcher's utter horror, it wasn't Billie Eilish that started to play but something else entirely. Minty had gone against his wishes. Well, of course she had. He'd been a fool to expect anything less from Minty Morrigan.

As the opening piano notes faded, Minty raised her chin and started to sing. It took Fletcher a moment to recognise the song. Had Chappell Roan ever envisioned a ninety-six-year-old Tinkerbell singing her LGBTQ anthem in an English village hall?

Minty's wavering voice gave the opening lyrics a certain poignancy. The audience was rapt.

Fletcher looked around the little theatre. All eyes were on Minty. A smile on every face. She had them in the palm of her hand. When she got to the chorus, the actors onstage joined in and the audience was on their feet. 'Pink Pony Club' had never felt so profound as it did at that moment. The sight brought tears to Fletcher's eyes. It had all been worth it. The rehearsals, the stresses, the sacrifices. It had all led to this beautiful, magnificent moment. Perhaps they'd do *Cinderella* next year.

As Minty came to the final rendition of the chorus, the tears were streaming down Fletcher's cheeks. His make-up would be a mess. He spotted May holding a tissue to her eyes on the front row. Cass had her arms in the air, laughing and singing along with Bastian. Cass's eyes opened wide as Minty rose into the air for the big finish. The applause was deafening. Well, not quite deafening, but definitely very loud.

Minty, bless her, continued to sing, swishing her skirt around as she hovered above the stage. Fletcher was overcome with love for everyone in the room as he looked up at Minty. She was the angel on top of the Christmas tree, the cherry on the cake, the–

Fletcher gasped and dove for the side of the stage, getting tangled up in his skirts on the way. As he tumbled over the edge, he hissed at the rigger. 'Get her down! Get her down NOW!'

At the after-party in The Crown, everyone was in high spirits. All except for Fletcher. He was sulking beside the fire, an ice pack held to his forehead, the dogs snoozing under the table.

'How could she forget her knickers?' he asked May.

'To be fair,' May said, 'she didn't forget. She never wears them. I'm surprised the rigger didn't say something.'

Minty was in a corner of the pub with Desi. They were

surrounded by admirers including a group of gentlemen from Demeter Gardens.

'I think he averted his eyes when he was dealing with Minty,' Fletcher replied. 'Poor lad, didn't know where to look with Minty sharing saucy stories from her past the whole time.'

'I don't think anyone beyond the first two rows could see anything,' May said soothingly. 'And anyone who did notice wasn't offended. They all know Minty. It's par for the course. Jean Drysdale said it was the funniest thing she'd seen in ages. And I thought Drew McCulloch was going to have a heart attack. It was probably the first fanny he'd seen in decades.'

Fletcher snorted, trying to stop himself from laughing. 'You should've seen my view.' He shook his head. 'It will haunt me for the rest of my days.'

'Put it in one of your books,' May said.

'No one would believe it,' Fletcher replied.

Cass joined them with a tray of glasses. 'Prosecco?'

'Not for me,' May said, moving away from them. Her smile had disappeared when Cass arrived. There was something going on between the two of them. Fletcher had sensed it at the panto. What had happened to make May so angry?

CHAPTER 46

HERE COMES SANTA CLAUS

May went to the bar to buy herself another G and T. The pub was buzzing with festive cheer. A group at one of the tables were all wearing red Santa hats. The waitress behind the bar had a sprig of mistletoe pinned in her hair. She regularly leant over the bar to receive a kiss on the cheek.

May felt like such a Scrooge amidst the merriment. She was still getting her head around the fact that her sister and her ex-husband had a child together. It all happened before May had met James, he and Cass had done nothing wrong in that respect. The seventies had been the time of Free Love. May had certainly had her own share of fun. The funny thing was, she didn't even remember James being at the Isle of Wight Festival. They hadn't met until the following year when they were back in Cambridge. The most astonishing part of it all was that Cass had kept the secret for so long.

May tried to sort through her emotions. She felt shock. She'd assumed the baby had been Jimi's. He and Cass had been insepara-ble the summer before he died. Cass had always said they were just friends though May had never quite believed it. She'd rather liked the idea of a Hendrix/Morrigan mash-up. Maybe the child and his or her offspring would be musical too.

But Faraday/Morrigan? It just made her feel sick. She'd wanted a child with James for so long. Did she feel jealous of Cass? Yes, if she was brutally honest with herself, some part of her envied Cass. She'd done something that May had dreamt about for years.

May also felt frustrated. She'd thought she was shot of him, had been glad for once that they'd never had a family. Now it looked like Greenway would end up in his hands after all, or at least in the hands of his child. It felt deeply unfair.

But this person, whoever they were, was a Morrigan too. That couldn't be denied.

Of course, May could choose to just let it lie. Cass would probably go along with that. May hadn't even told Fletcher about this particularly grisly detail yet. No one would be the wiser. It would be her and Cass's secret. Greenway would go to the council. May would be dead, so what did it matter?

But she would never let that happen. Whether she liked it or not, May knew she would follow this story to the bitter end. It was in her nature, which couldn't be denied for long.

Minty was at the end of the bar with her entourage. 'Young Chloe suggested the song. I thought it was a wonderful choice, so heartfelt. We must include some Chappell Roan at the next Demeter dance. Have you listened to 'Casual'? So naughty!' Minty was in her element.

'Are you okay?' Cass joined May at the bar. She'd swapped the Prosecco for a bottle of Peroni.

May tensed, then slouched with a sigh. 'I will be,' she said. 'Why didn't you tell me you knew James before I met him?'

'I didn't really know him. It was just that week,' Cass said. 'He was at the festival with someone I knew from Cambridge. I can't believe *he* never mentioned it.'

May's eyes opened wide. 'Oh my God!' She put her hand to

her mouth. 'The night we met at the Blue Boar, he came over and said, "So, we meet again". I've always thought it was just a cheesy pick-up line, that he was trying to be funny.' She looked at Cass. 'All those years. Did he think I was the girl he'd met at the festival?'

'But I would've told him my name,' Cass said. She screwed up her face. 'Or did I? We were off our faces the whole week. Maybe I didn't.' She shrugged. 'The next time I saw him, you were already married. I thought it best to pretend it had never happened, but I guess that was just what was best for me. I'm sorry.'

May squeezed her sister's hand. 'I understand why you did what you did,' she said. 'Who's to say I might not have done the same? Did you ever tell him about the pregnancy?'

'God, no!' The idea seemed repugnant to Cass. 'I didn't even like him that much. He was just part of the craziness of the festival. He seemed like the type who would pressure me to keep the baby, but I'd already made my mind up about that. I didn't need his input.'

'Yes,' May agreed. 'He probably would've done that.' She looked up at Cass. 'Do you think he eventually worked it out? That when he realised I wasn't the woman he thought I was, that's when he started the affair?'

'Even if that's true,' Cass said, 'none of it is your fault. *You* didn't know. And, if he did stop loving you, he should've had the balls to leave, not keep you dangling for years. He didn't want you, but he didn't want anyone else to have you. He's a wanker.'

'I'll drink to that,' May replied, raising her glass.

'I'm glad you know now,' Cass said. She leant in closer. 'This doesn't have to go any further though. It can end here, with us.'

'I considered that,' May said. Cass smelt of Calvin Klein's Obsession. She'd worn the same fragrance since they were teens. The familiar scent felt like a hug. 'I think we both know that's not going to happen.'

Cass rolled her eyes, then looked over May's shoulder. 'Here comes trouble,' she said before stepping away to blend into the group surrounding Minty.

May turned to find DCI Armstrong standing beside her holding a pint of Guinness. 'Your mother's quite the performer,' he said. 'Does that talent run in the family?'

May looked over at Minty. She'd rarely seen her mother so happy.

'You enjoyed the show?' May asked.

He nodded. 'Hadn't been to a panto in years, though I was technically working.'

'Sure you were,' May said. 'I think you were there for the music. I saw you singing along. How on earth do you know so much popular music?'

He chuckled. 'Grandchildren. They listen to it constantly. I pick it up by osmosis.'

'Osmosis, is it?' May said. 'Who sounds like a dictionary now?' He was standing so close his arm was pressed against hers. 'I guess you'll be spending Christmas with them. The holidays must be lovely with children.'

He shook his head, then took a sip of his beer. 'They're with my daughter-in-law's family in Oz this year. It's just me, myself and I for Christmas.' He moved even closer. 'I think what I actually said is that you talk like a thesaurus.'

'Encyclopaedia,' May corrected.

He nodded, looking at her eyes, her mouth. 'Ah, yes. That's right. Let me buy you another drink, May Morrigan.'

CHAPTER 47

HALLELUJAH

May adjusted a sparkling earring and looked at herself in the mirror over her dresser. She smoothed the black velvet of her dress. It was always nice to dress up for Christmas Day.

'Still got it,' she whispered, winking at her glowing reflection, then turned and headed downstairs.

Pots and pans banged in the kitchen. Fletcher's voice was raised over the racket. 'No, not like that! You're whipping cream, not churning butter!'

'All right, all right,' Armstrong's deep voice replied. 'Like this?'

'Here, let me do it,' Cass said.

May pivoted and headed towards the library. Minty and Desi sat side by side on the little sofa, staring into the fire, half-empty glasses of Buck's Fizz in front of them on the table. The dogs were curled up on their cushion, worryingly close to the flames. Desi swiped at her eyes as May sat down across from them.

May raised an eyebrow. 'Feeling melancholy? On Christmas morning? The holidays can have that effect sometimes.'

Minty sighed, still watching the flames. 'I think it's time we told you everything.' She turned to look at May.

May considered raising a hand to stop Minty, saying she didn't want to know. The problem was that she did want to know. May wanted to know everything.

Desi cleared her throat. 'Thank you for disposing of that knife for me.' She fiddled with a ring on one hand. May noticed it was a Claddagh, like the one in the photograph. 'Do you remember my daughter, Dido… and what happened?'

'Of course,' May replied softly. 'I have fond memories of Dido.' She cast her mind back, seeing a cheerful girl with long red hair. 'Wasn't there a love affair that went sour? Isn't that why she left London, then came home and…' She stopped, reliving the shock of the news. It had seemed impossible for someone so young and vibrant to choose to end her own life.

Desi nodded. 'The affair was with Clark Wolfe.'

'Clark? But he must've been…' May did the math. 'Over twenty years older than her. Dido was barely out of her teens.'

'That was Clark all over wasn't it.' Minty sipped her drink, found the glass empty and set it down with a sigh. 'Dido was costume assistant on that film, the one he was convinced would win him an Oscar but ended up going straight to video. What was it? Something Gothic with a lot of wool.'

'*Jane Eyre*,' Desi said.

Why had May recently been thinking about *Jane Eyre*?

'The affair started then. He was married to the Spanish actress at the time, what's-her-name? The one with the lips,' Minty continued.

A coal tumbled in the fire, releasing sparks onto the hearth. May leant forward to dust a tiny smoking ember from George's fur. George remained oblivious, drunk with warmth and contentment. 'I had no idea about Clark and Dido,' she said.

'Neither did I,' Desi said. 'At least, not until recently. I packed away all of Dido's things right after… you know. When I moved into the care home a few months ago and went through the boxes, I found Dido's journals. She'd kept them since she was a wee child. I read every single one of them. It was like having her back for a while.' Desi gave a long sigh before continuing in a quieter voice. 'Then, in the last diary, were the details of the affair. Falling in love for the first time… the joy and excitement… then the surprise of the pregnancy… the heartache.'

'Pregnancy? Oh, poor Dido,' May said, her face tight with sorrow. She closed her eyes, the fire suddenly too bright. May knew all too well the difficulties of being a young woman dealing with an unwanted pregnancy. She thought of Cass too, and everything she'd been through. 'I'm sure Clark was absolutely charming about that.'

'That's why she did it,' Minty said.

May sighed. 'Poor, poor Dido. Clark was not worth it.'

Minty looked at her. 'Not Dido. *Desi*. That's why Desi… and I… did what we did.'

May opened her eyes. 'What did you do?' She'd asked the question, though in her heart she knew what they were going to say.

'I killed Clark,' Desi said, raising her chin. 'And I'd do it again.'

'And I helped,' Minty added.

The fire crackled as the three women sat silently, each of them seeing ghosts amongst the flames. Then May nodded slowly. 'I knew something was off about the two of you finding his body. I just didn't know what it was.'

'Dido's journals told the whole story,' Desi said. 'Clark's cruelty, how she'd gone to Broadstairs to keep the pregnancy a secret, leaving the baby on the steps of St Mary's Chapel. You know what Dido was like, once she'd made up her mind about something, there was no turning back. She planned her death as efficiently as she did everything else in her little life.'

'The steps of the chapel? But… my God.' That's why she'd been thinking of *Jane Eyre*; the quote on the back of the photograph tucked into the blanket with Caspar.

'Yes. Exactly.' Minty tutted, placing a hand on Desi's. 'Such a tragedy all round.'

'Caspar learnt that Clark was probably his father,' Desi said. 'He'd found a relative through some kind of DNA thing, then worked out the rest. That's why he met Clark that morning on the heath, and it's why Clark killed him. He was afraid of the scandal, convinced he'd be portrayed as the next Jimmy Savile.'

'But Dido wasn't a minor,' May replied.

'God only knows what skeletons Clark Wolfe had hiding in his capacious closet,' Minty said. 'He didn't want a bunch of journalists opening that door and poking around.'

'Caspar tried to explain that he wasn't interested in scandal, that he only wanted to know about his parents, but Clark didn't believe him,' Desi continued. 'He was certain the details would get out, then his career would be finished once and for all.' Desi shook her head. 'Clark didn't even know Dido was Caspar's mother. She wasn't the only one to find herself in such a state because of Clark Wolfe. Poor Caspar died without even knowing his mother's name or that his grandmother was right here in Blackheath. Killed by his own father.'

'It's like a Greek tragedy,' May said.

A champagne cork popped, and voices cheered, causing them to jump. May was reminded that a detective chief inspector was whipping cream in her kitchen. She lowered her voice. 'How do you know all this?'

Minty squirmed under her gaze, but Desi remained defiant. 'I had him in my room at Demeter Gardens. I asked him there for a fitting, drugged his tea and tied him to a wheelchair. I wanted him to understand the pain he'd caused before I killed him. Not that he gave a tinker's toss. He talked about it with pride. How women couldn't resist him and it wasn't his fault if they fell pregnant, the dozy mares. The man really was a horrible monster.'

'But, where did you get the drugs and the wheelchair?' May would never have guessed that sweet Desi had it in her.

The two older women rolled their eyes. 'It's a care home, dear,' Desi replied. 'A virtual drug emporium. You can get anything you want from the residents. Uppers, downers, laxatives, sleeping pills. You just need to know who to ask.'

May filed this information away for future use.

'Once I realised he was incapable of remorse, I gave him a stronger dose of the sleeping pills, then...' Desi made a stabbing motion, causing her bracelets to jingle. 'He made it so easy, still had the knife in his coat pocket. Then we wheeled him out onto the heath and dumped him.' She dusted her hands together.

'I was going to get in the chair so Desi could push it back to the care home, but we were interrupted by that odd man and had to improvise.'

'Such a fuss,' Desi said.

'I was meant to leave the knife with the body. Then that man started shouting. I got so flustered, I put it in my handbag. I knew you'd know what to do with it,' Minty said, smiling at May.

The noises in the kitchen had calmed. May imagined the turkey, removed from its briny bath, rubbed with butter, roasting in the hot oven. Fletcher, Cass, Bastian and Gus were probably sitting at the pine kitchen table peeling potatoes and scoring sprouts in boozy camaraderie.

May picked up the empty glasses, moved to the drinks trolley and made fresh glasses of Buck's Fizz before rejoining Minty and Desi in front of the fire.

'This stays between us,' May said, looking at Minty. 'No showing off at the care home, boasting about how you helped Desi get rid of Clark Wolfe, understand?'

'As if I'd do such a thing,' Minty replied.

'At first, I didn't care if I was caught,' Desi said. 'I did it for Dido and how many years do I have left anyway? Then Fletcher showed me the blanket. I recognised her work immediately.' Desi buried her face in a tissue. 'If only I'd acted sooner. I had a grandson. Even if he was half Clark Wolfe, I wish I'd had the chance to know him.'

'You still have a great-granddaughter,' May said quietly. 'You need to stick around for her.'

CHAPTER 48

MERRY XMAS EVERYBODY

May looked around the table in Greenway's rarely used dining room. She and Cass had set the table with their grandmother's 1930s Berkeley china. The red-and-gold pattern was perfect for Christmas lunch. Fletcher had outdone himself, producing a golden turkey and plate after plate of delicious side dishes. Plus gravy, and both cranberry and bread sauces. The platters were now half-empty while their bellies were overfull. Remnants of the Christmas crackers littered the floor around them.

Minty sat at the head of the table in her purple paper crown with a daughter on each side of her. Wizzard could be heard playing on the radio in the kitchen. 'Roll me into the other room,' Minty said. 'I'm too full to walk.'

'I was just going to suggest a nice digestive walk around the heath,' Cass said to groans from the table. She was wearing a Zandra Rhodes dress that May recognised from her own wardrobe.

'I may never walk again,' Fletcher replied. 'God, I feel smashed. One of you must've spiked my drink.'

'All six of them?' Desi asked.

Armstrong stifled a yawn. 'I think I need a nap. Doesn't turkey have something in it that makes you sleepy?'

'Tryptophan,' Bastian replied, covering his own yawn.

'We haven't opened the gifts.' Minty clapped her hands together. 'To the tree!'

The group reconvened in the library armed with mugs of strong coffee laced with Bailey's. May curled up on the small sofa beside Armstrong while Fletcher distributed the presents. There were chocolates and socks. Perfumes and scarves. A new board game. A new book. A hat. An umbrella. The dachshunds were rolling in the tissue paper scattered on the floor when Fletcher yelped, 'May! You didn't.' He held up a sheet of paper.

'They don't do actual tickets anymore,' she said. 'Which makes for a pretty underwhelming gift, but I hope you don't mind.'

'Mind?' he said. 'This is wonderful. How did you know I was thinking of going?'

May shook her head. 'I didn't. After all the work for the panto, you deserve to get away and I know you've been missing him desperately.'

'Tickets for what?' Minty asked.

Fletcher held up the piece of paper. 'I'm going to Chennai for New Year.' He looked at the paper again. 'Tomorrow! I need to pack.' He jumped up. 'I'm going to ring Sparks and let him know.'

May laid her head on the arm of the sofa. Slade was playing on the radio in the kitchen. Poor Dido, giving up her baby like that. And poor Cass, who'd felt it necessary to do the same thing. As someone who'd wanted children but never had them, May found the idea of this sacrifice particularly painful. It was too late for Caspar, but maybe there was a Morrigan out there who was looking for his or her family.

May hadn't told Cass yet, but when she booked Fletcher's tickets to India she'd also booked two tickets to Houston in the new year. Cass would argue, she always did, but she'd come round in the end. If there was a Morrigan out there, May and Cass would find them. Even if it meant going to Texas.

May jumped when Cass pulled a party popper, showering her and Armstrong with streamers. The holidays really were for children. May leant over to remove the water pistol she'd hidden under the sofa. 'Cass Morrigan, I'd like to have a word with you about my Rose's chocolates,' she said. Cass shrieked and ran from the room with May in hot pursuit.

Thankfully, everyone's a child at Christmas.

ACKNOWLEDGEMENTS

This book was a particular labour of love as it was written during a very challenging year. Huge thanks to Betsy Reavley and Fred Freeman for their support and patience.

Thanks as ever to my wonderful editor, Ian Skewis, for his kind encouragement, gentle corrections and eagle eye. It's such a comfort knowing my book is in his capable hands.

To my friends and family, thank you, thank you, thank you. I can see light at the end of the tunnel.

A special thanks to the partners who love and support some of my favourite women. Jim, Kieran, and Sophia, thank you for understanding when I needed them the most. Love you guys.

With gratitude to Matt and the team at Halcyon Books in Lee where so much of this book was written, fuelled by your excellent coffee and warm atmosphere.

This book is dedicated to my brother and sister. We're bound by blood and memories and just enough childhood trauma that we can still laugh about it. I love you both and, Jon, I'm sorry for tormenting you. There, it's in writing now.

With huge love to my amazing kids who are setting off on their own life adventures. Never forget you can always, always come home.

Listen to *A Most Curious Christmas* playlist on Spotify.
For updates, bonus chapters and more, join the mailing list at kjblack.com.

A NOTE FROM THE PUBLISHER

Thank you for reading this book. If you enjoyed it please do consider leaving a review on Amazon to help others find it too.

We hate typos. All of our books have been rigorously edited and proofread, but sometimes mistakes do slip through. If you have spotted a typo, please do let us know and we can get it amended within hours.

info@bloodhoundbooks.com

www.ingramcontent.com/pod-product-compliance
Lightning Source LLC
Chambersburg PA
CBHW050616190726
48283CB00007B/2448